For Dad a

Acknowledgements

I'd like to thank Clare and the boys for all of their help and support over the years.
I wouldn't be here without you...

Factory Fortnight

Chapter One
Let the holidays begin

York
July 1978

A low morning mist hung over the City, rising from the river that curved its way along the flood plains and through, into the centre, with the only noise coming from birdsong and the rattle of bottles on the back of milk floats as they hummed their way back to the depots.

The sun was already bright, although the heat had not yet hit the pavements, as workers making their way to shifts strode briskly forward, or pedalled reluctantly, coughing, chatting and laughing towards the factories dotted about the city

Standing on the bridge of Wigginton road, the huge ornate wooden clock that sat on the apex clicked noisily every minute, shaking the notices placed beneath it, advertising vacancies at the factory. Under the bridge, the 5.40am from Selby belched diesel fumes, idling on the railway line, having discharged the morning shift and waiting patiently for the night shift to climb aboard. The smell of cocoa was prevalent in the air, the gentle breeze mixing it with the tang of peppermint, creating an instant taste sensation that permeated the city, allowing all to smell it, regardless of where they lived.

The clock's minute hand clicked its final journey of the hour and the sound of the factory hooter called out the hour of 6am. Any change to the scenery wasn't immediate but slowly, a noise began rising from beyond the factory gates as they squealed open and the first few cyclists came through them, turning left and right, waving goodbyes and the occasional shouted, abusive remark. But quickly, the dribble of those few soon turned into a torrent, the crescendo of noise rising as a mass of cyclists poured forth from the factory gates, followed by walkers, the women with linked arms and older men ambling through, as they all began a synchronised lighting of cigarettes, creating a mushroom cloud of nicotine smoke that engulfed the security guards in their watch-huts, as they all poured through the ornate iron gates.

Roger Brown pushed hard on the pedals of his bike as he made his way over the bridge with his oldest friend, Sid. Both of them had cigarettes dangling at the corners of their mouths, already half-smoked as they reached the downward slope, that led towards the city centre. They stopped pedalling and freewheeled down.

It was beginning to warm up already and the early mist was quickly evaporating as they turned sharply right, shouting their goodbyes to the rest of the workers, as they all splintered off in different directions.

Roger and Sid pedalled along a lane, past the newly built hospital that towered over everything surrounding it, before they jumped off their bikes as they came to the footbridge over the railway. They hoisted the bikes over their shoulders and trotted up the steps and down the other side, panting a little with the effort. At the bottom of the footbridge, they climbed back on their bikes and paused to light another cigarette.

Taking out a packet of Regal from his breast pocket, Roger lit two and handed one to Sid.

"Cheers, mate." He sucked on it a couple of times before taking it out. Before them stood the rows of soot-blackened terraced houses that were lined up beyond the railway line. They paused a while and puffed in companionable silence. Around them, people were starting to emerge from the streets, all heading to work. Roger and Sid recognised most of them, waving and nodding in greeting.

"Are we out tonight?" Roger took the cigarette from the corner of his mouth and gently spat a thread of tobacco into the gutter.

"Aye, I think we are." Sid replied. "I need to give in the balance for next week."

Roger raised his eyebrows. "You still not done that yet? Bloody hell, lad. You're cutting it fine."

"I know but I still had the balance on that new suite that Bab's bought, didn't I?" Sid grimaced at his friend.

Roger smiled at him, knowingly.

"We'd only had the old one twenty-years."

Roger laughed and coughed at the same time.

"Well, she's been patient."

"Aye, but with the fortnight coming up. I've better things to spend me money on."

Behind them, the Scarborough train rattled past, on its way into the station. Both turned to watch it pass.

"I can't wait to get to the coast, me." Roger spoke wistfully. "Four weeks of night-shifts, I'm ready for the break." He coughed aggressively and spat again, into the gutter.

"Yeah, I know what you mean" He looked at Roger who was watching the train disappear from view. "Are you bringing the lads this year?"

Roger turned to look at him and, throwing his cigarette end into the gutter, he smiled. "You're joking aren't you? It's time those buggers stood on their own two feet" He turned and threw his left leg over the cross bar of his bike and drew the pedal up with the top of his foot. "Right, I'm off fella. I'll see you tonight." He pushed down and was off towards his street.

"Right mate!" Sid raised his arm in salute and shouted after him. "Sleep tight!"

Roger lifted his hand in the air in response and, without looking back, he turned the corner and was gone.

He pedalled into the top of the street and then turned sharply into the alley that ran along the back of the houses, avoiding the deep central gulley that ran along the middle that was high with weeds and hidden dog shit.

He rolled to a halt outside the back gate to his house, using his hand to stop himself along the brickwork. The brakes that he'd been meaning to fix for years would squeal loudly, echoing down the alley and he didn't want to wake his wife too early, as it really wasn't worth the hassle.

He quietly lifted the latch to the back yard and rolled his bike through, pushing it by the seat underneath the white laundry on the line that had been drying overnight. The yard contained several flower pots, spilling out sweet peas and geranium flowers. Two tomato plants were pinned to the south-facing wall in a bid to ripen the fruit but the heat had only served to wizen them into defeat.

Four bikes, each one positioned in an order of retrieval, depending upon shifts at the factory, were stacked on top of one another against the wall and Roger lifted the other three, rolling his underneath them. He didn't want waking by the others collecting their bikes to go to work.

As Roger bent to remove his trouser clips, he looked up to the bedroom window and saw that the curtains were still drawn to the room in which his sons slept.

"Lazy bastards" he muttered under his breath, his eye catching that of Mrs Whiting, their next-door neighbour, who was watching him from her window. He smiled up at her, but no smile was returned. She dropped her net curtain in disdain, but he could still see her behind it; watching him.

"Nosey fucking cow" he muttered, as he bent to take his trouser leg from out of his sock. Straightening up, he walked to the wooden back door, pushed it open and stepped up into the kitchen.

His first view was of the cat, sitting on the draining board of the sink, drinking from the kitchen tap and then the detritus of last night from his two sons, Michael and James. Fish and chip wrappers lay scrunched and discarded across the worktops and used glasses filled the sink. The bin was full of Skol beer bottles and a few that hadn't made the bin, rested on the lino of the kitchen floor.

"For fuck's sake!" He muttered.

Roger took in the view of the kitchen, cursed again and began clearing up, shooing the cat away from the sink, it meowed its discontent at him before promptly sitting on the floor to lick itself.

The kitchen was small with some pale cream melamine units fixed to the walls, next to an old dresser that contained his wife's best china, with a sink and an upright oven facing each other opposite the window. It sat between the living room of the small terraced house and the bathroom that had been put in as an extension when the boys were born. A staircase to the upper floor led from the kitchen, beneath which, a small, pull-out table was sat, every space in the house utilised to make best use of it.

Above the sink, the window to the kitchen overlooked the back yard, showing the washing hung idly, limp, without any breeze to move it.

As he began emptying the bin, he heard movement from upstairs, his wife's footsteps across the landing and the start of her descent down the stairs. She always used his home-coming as an alarm call when he was on night shift and, as she stepped down into the kitchen, she sniffed the air and then saw the mess that Roger was trying to clear.

"Jesus" she said, walking past him towards the bathroom at the other end of the kitchen. Closing the door behind her, Roger heard the taps go on and the noise of her morning ritual.

"Morning" he muttered and carried the bin bag to the yard. He stopped after placing the bag in the metal can, quietly replacing the lid in case Mrs Whiting next door started moaning about the noise again and he looked up at the sky, breathing deeply. The smell of chocolate wafted across the city; it was everywhere, his clothes, his hair and in the air. There was no escape.

He could hear his wife, Maureen, brushing her teeth from behind the frosted glass of the bathroom window, getting ready to begin her shift and, faintly, he could hear the stirrings of his two boys in their room, waking up to start their day too. The sky was already a bright blue, meaning another hot summer's day and he hoped he slept better than he had for the past few nights, his last night shift before going on holiday after the weekend.

He felt exhausted, his eyes were burning slightly from tiredness and he recognised the first pangs of hunger now he had finished. Breakfast and bed; that was what he needed.

Maureen came out of the bathroom, wafting talcum powder and a faint whiff of lavender behind her, she was still in her nightdress, her slippered feet shuffling across the lino as she reached behind Roger for the kettle and leaned into the sink.

"How was your shift?" she asked, the metal lid squeaking as she twisted it free, a satisfying plop given, before it was rammed beneath the tap for filling.

"S'alright" he replied, turning to look at his wife, her face shiny from being washed, her short, curled hair catching the light from the kitchen window.

"Do you want a brew?" She asked as she lit the gas and placed the dented kettle on the hob.

"Please", he replied, he waited for something further from her but realised he wasn't going to get anything, so reached into the fridge for some bacon.

"I see the lads were out again last night?" He asked, lifting a frying pan onto the hob. He clicked an igniter and the whoosh of flames hit the bottom of the pan.

"I think they got in about half-eleven." She said. They were talking and tasking, performing a light-footed, intricate dance around the galley kitchen, knowing instinctively where the other one was.

Roger reached into the fridge again, lifting out a block of dripping whilst Maureen passed her arm under his, taking out the milk bottle.

"They're always out on the piss. There'll be nowt left for their holidays at this rate" The smell of hot fat filled the kitchen as Roger swirled the hard, white fat around the pan.

"They'll be right" said Maureen dismissively, splashing milk into two mugs.

"And don't you be subbing 'em" retorted Roger, waving a lard-encrusted knife in her direction. He unwrapped the bacon from the wax paper and peeled off three rashers, laying them reverently in the pan, the back-fat sizzling and curling as it touched the heat. "I know you give 'em back rent when they're short. Time they stood on their own two feet."

Maureen said nothing, merely sighed slightly and shook her head, looking wistfully out of the window as she mashed the tea bags in the pot and mouthed silently back at him, two words, which, had he seen, he would easily have interpreted as 'piss-off'.

Upstairs, Michael and James were stirring. A strong shaft of light was breaking through the curtains, illuminating the dust motes in the air being disturbed by the lifting and throwing back of sheets.

Michael, the older of the two brothers by one year, sat up and reached for a glass of water as he tried to dislodge his tongue from the roof of his mouth. Nothing. He could have sworn he'd brought a glass to bed the night before, he hadn't been that pissed, he thought, but he looked around, at the bedside table, the floor: nothing.

He heard James starting to move and looked over towards his brother and saw the glass he'd brought up, by his brother's bed.

"Bastard" he muttered.

Standing up, he reached for his jeans and slipped them on. He was tall, lean and blonde, his hair curling down over his neck, he ran a hand through it, swept it back on top and let it fall back over his eyes. He brushed the fine down on his chest and wished it were hairier, something worth opening his shirt for when looking for girls. He was bursting for a pee and a drink. As he walked past his brother's bed, he kicked the mattress and pulled back the sheets.

"Up!" he shouted and walked out, leaving his brother muttering and blindly reaching for the covers.

Out on the landing, he could hear his parents talking and the smell of bacon and hot lard reached his nostrils.

Fantastic, some breakfast, he thought as he padded down the stairs in his bare feet.

"Morning" he said, his throat rasping over last night's beer and cigarettes.

"Morning love" said Maureen, she stood on her tiptoes to peck him on the cheek and, reaching for another mug she went to pour her son a drink.

"Bloody state this kitchen was this morning" said Roger, not returning the greeting, flipping the rashers in the pan. When he turned to look at his son, he only heard the bathroom lock being run home and no one standing there.

"Toss-pot" he muttered under his breath.

By the time Michael came out of the bathroom, his dad was cracking a couple of eggs into the pan next to the bacon. He pulled a t-shirt over his head and walked to where his dad was standing.

"Can you put some in for us Dad, please? I'm starving" said Michael, leaning over, close to his dad, to look at the food.

"Get your bloody own, you lazy sod," replied Roger, "I'm having this, then off to bed"

Roger sniffed the air near his son's face. "You smell like a friggin' brewery"

Michael smiled and reached for his tea, raised it to his lips, while his mother was trying to put sugar in as he drank.

"Cheers Mam" slurping loudly, he carried on watching his Dad making breakfast. "Ah, go on Dad. Just put something in the pan and I'll finish it off when I get down".

"Bugger off! Get your own." He snarled at him, turned to face him and, not for the first time, realised he had to look up at his own son. "Bloody bottles and wrappers all over this kitchen last night, my lad." He spoke whilst waving his fork in the air in front of Michael's face. "I don't need that after a night shift, do I?"

Michael looked at his father and smiled. "No Dad, you don't."

"Thank you" replied Roger.

"I'm sorry Dad" Michael turned to his mum and grinned, flicking his hair back from his eyes and rolling his eyes. She gave a smile of resignation in response.

"Mind you are" Roger splashed fat over the egg yolks to set them. Finishing, he served it all up with a flourish onto a plate, laying buttered bread next to it all.

He scooped up plate, cutlery, tea and the bottle of brown sauce and went to the small table that was tucked under the stairs in the corner of the kitchen and sat opposite his wife, who looked at his plate, muttered under her breath and went to make some toast.

"What were you doing out on a Thursday night, anyway?" He asked, letting the muttered comment go, "I thought you were saving your money." Roger wrapped bacon in bread and dipped it into the egg.

Michael watched the yellow yolk burst all over his dad's plate, scooped up on the bread, then into his father's mouth. He couldn't help but salivate.

"It wasn't a big night" he said, turning to cut a slice of bread. He smothered it in butter and began wiping it around the hot pan his father had just used, picking up bits of bacon and egg white, along with the hot dripping. "We were celebrating" he said, speaking through a mouthful of bread.

"Get a plate" Maureen said, slapping his arm. "What were you celebrating, love?"

"If it's not six score draws, I don't want to hear it" said Roger, chewing his breakfast.

"Factory fortnight Dad. Two weeks of sun, sea and" he paused, "stuff" Michael licked his fingers, then wiped them on his jeans.

"Not if you've pissed all your money up the bloody wall, you're not." Muttered Roger, looking at the clock on the wall, "and not if you don't get your arse and your brother, out of this bloody house and off to work!"

"Shut up you" snapped Maureen. "Give him a chance."

Roger grumbled into his plate, slurping tea to wash his bread down. Maureen sat down again, a plate of buttered white bread, with jam, stacked on a plate, which she put on the table with some force, causing the crockery to rattle. Michael put down his mug on the side and went to take a slice of the bread. His father instinctively, wrapped his arm around his plate, defending his food.

"Dad?" Michael spoke softly, still chewing.

"No" Said Roger.

Michael sighed and, letting his head drop backwards, he spoke to the ceiling.

"I've not asked you anything!" He exclaimed

"If it's money; it's a no"

"Well it's not money" He sighed again, looked at his mum and frowned. Maureen merely looked back and shook her head lightly, as if to say: 'you'll get nothing from him'.

"I'd best get ready for work." Michael moved in a dejected manner to leave the kitchen.

Roger's eyes followed his son as he climbed the stairs, slowly. He looked at Maureen who was staring at him, looking disapprovingly at her husband. He sighed.

"What is it?" He called after his son.

Michael paused and leant over the bannister to look at his mum and dad.

"Can I borrow your tent that's in the shed?"

Silence.

Michael paused, nodded to his mother and took his opportunity to go and get dressed.

Roger looked at Maureen with a fork that had bacon and dripping egg speared on it, on its way to his mouth.

"Tent?"

Chapter Two
Factory Life

Slim dipped his hand into the white paper bag marked 'waste' and pulled out a slightly disfigured chocolate bar, looked around to check if anyone was watching, before popping it whole, into his mouth.

He was standing in his overalls in the vast, cavernous space of the warehouse, wondering which pallet to check off next, the list on his manifest running to several pages, as, by the roller shutters, fork lift trucks chugged backwards and forwards, moving the towers of boxes in and out.

"Eating again, young Brook?" Eric Anderson, the shift supervisor, swept past Slim by his right shoulder, causing him to spin around in surprise at being caught.

"Just a snack Mr Anderson!" He called after him, watching his boss' white-coated back disappear into the warehouse shadows, the only light coming from tiny windows in the eaves of the ceiling, shining in shafts like a church.

Slim sighed, blowing several little pieces of semi-chewed chocolate out, swallowed and walked back over to the boxes he was supposed to be arranging before loading.

The part of store he was working in had become steadily emptied, in readiness for factory fortnight shut-down. Other spaces were being filled to the rafters with cases, ready for the Christmas confectionary that would be started after the break, which were demarcated, wrapped and sealed.

A light breeze came through the warehouse door, twisting packing paper that had worked loose, folding itself under its own weight as it worked its way along the walls where they met the floor.

It was gratefully cool, the redbrick of the walls absorbing the heat from the summer sun on the outside, the packages of flavourings and milk powder remaining in peak condition within their cocoon. Trucks would come regularly, but even now they were few and far between, the final week before shut-down, everyone was cleaning down, finishing off ready for their holidays.

Slim was almost as wide as he was tall, Andrew Brook by name but he hadn't gone by that for many years since expanding rapidly at the age of eight. Everyone had told him it was just puppy fat but adolescence came and went and he remained a solid mass, only marginally taller. His short dark hair only accentuated the roundness of his face, pushed under his regulation-cap with his ruddy cheeks pushed out in a sigh as he realised how much work he still had to do.

He disliked working in the warehouse, with all of his friends either up in the factory on engineering or in the packing rooms, with all their camaraderie and egos and especially, near all of the women. His father had got him this job straight from school, believing that distribution would offer more in terms of progression. It hadn't.

Both his parents had worked here, had met there in fact and his father was still here as a Charge Hand, hence why it was expected for him to follow his dad into the factory. There were high hopes for Slim but hopes were fading as, at nearly 20 years old, he was neither promoted, married or any further forward than he had been at 16.

He looked at the remaining packing boxes in front of him and sighed again. He had until lunch time to stack them onto pallets and wrap them, ready for transport.

Two floors up, James and Billy were adjusting the conveyors on the wafer lines, shouting to each other over the noise of the machinery.

James, the younger brother to Michael, was coming to the end of his apprenticeship in the engineering team, working alongside Michael's best friend from school, Billy. He was smaller than his brother and dark, like his dad, but had been with the factory since he left school just before his sixteenth birthday, like most of his friends. Their tool kits by their feet, they both wore the blue overalls of the engineers, standing out from the hundreds of white coated factory workers that handled chocolate, most of them women and girls, to whom his eyes strayed every few minutes, hoping they were watching them as they worked.

The room was vast, with large windows, their blinds lowered, allowed the daylight in in shafts, illuminating segments of the floor, plunging everywhere else into darkness.

The conveyors that ran the length of the room, moving biscuits under chocolate enrobing machines, had been moved across the floor, away from the direct sunlight, the summer heat turning chocolate white, sending them to the waste pile.

Wooden floors were highly polished, scrubbed and varnished every year, washed four times a day, the wafer biscuits continuously sending a fine dust onto the floor in which James and Billy now lay, their tool kits beside them, as they tried to correct the calibration on the machines.

"Soon be here" James called, lifting his head, eyes level with a thousand wafers swarming by.

"What?" Billy shouted back. He tightened the socket some more and saw a couple of chocolate bars jump.

"Factory fortnight," replied James, "not long now"

"And what's that to us?" Billy slackened the nut again slightly, the conveyor smoothing out. "We can't afford to go, can we?"

Billy was the embodiment of style, even in his overalls, he looked fit and lean, handsome and affable, and everybody loved him and wanted to be near him. He wore his hair longer than most at the factory and was always being told to cut it and shave his sideburns but Billy could just smile and get away with things others would have their pay docked for.

The girls working at the end of the lines, packing boxes, were watching him and giggling, something he was more than aware of but was playing it cool.

As they were working, an Overseer walked up behind them, looking at their work or, more likely, looking at Billy knelt on the floor.

"Will you lads be finished soon?" said George Rivers, a tall, slightly effeminate man in his late fifties, he looked down on Billy who turned onto one knee and looked back up at George.

"In time for lunch. Mr Rivers" smiled Billy, "No bother" George couldn't help but smile back, he'd always had a soft spot for Billy and Billy knew it.

"Are you on the trip for Brid' next week lads?" George addressed both of them but was directing it all to Billy.

"Er, yes Mr Rivers, we are" James shouted from across the conveyor, trying to get the Overseer's attention. Billy looked at James, frowning.

"I didn't see your names on the bus lists. Who are you going with?" George ran his finger in some of the wafer dust, making a mental note to have his girls clean it all before the end of shift.

"We're making our own way there" Replied Billy, nodding at the overseer but still wearing a confused look on his face as he glanced back to James.

"That's a shame" cooed George, attention firmly back on Billy, "we were going to have a couple of stops along the way for a drink."

"Well, we'll be having a few stops ourselves, like" said Billy, returning to the socket set under the conveyor. "Cos, I don't know how the frig we'll be in Brid'" he muttered to himself.

James continued smiling at George, desperate to be noticed as a hard worker.

"Well, we'll have to have a drink when you're in Bridlington then. I'm sure all my girls" he turned to where his packing team were working, who all quickly looked away and busy as he did, "will all be waiting to see you."

As will I, he thought, but didn't say it. Smiling at them, George turned on his heel, and walked back to his lofty chair overlooking the ladies on the packing machine.

"Dirty auld bastard" muttered James.

"Ah, he's harmless" replied Billy "he wouldn't hurt a fly. Wouldn't know how to." He looked again at James, who was still grinning inanely. "So how are we going to be going for drinks with him and his girls if we aren't bloody well going?"

"I've an idea." James said, shuffling his way a little closer to his friend. "Well, it's mine and Michael's really."

"Which is?" Billy had returned to peering under the conveyor, trying to see if there was any more tension available in the belt.

"Well," said James, spelling it out like a teacher to a very thick child, "We can't afford the bus trip…"

"Do I really need to hear this?"

"And we can't afford the full board digs…"

"You're starting to get on my tits now, mate."

"But we get paid tonight…"

Billy put down his wrench with some force on the floor, causing both wafer dust and James to jump.

"Can you get to the frigging point!"

"We go camping!" James looked like he'd uncovered a hidden truth, his face lighting up and his eyes shining. Billy just stared at him.

"What 'y think?" He looked expectantly at his friend.

Billy took a deep breath and, gently retrieving his wrench from where it laid, he held it up, studied it, before replying, calmly.

"I think I'm going to shove this up your arse."

"Come on Billy! It's perfect! We only need enough for food and drink and, let's face it, we can probably do it better and a damn sight cheaper than being in a boarding house."

"Camping." The statement was all Billy could repeat.

"It's just somewhere to kip down between drinking sessions." James could see his friend thinking it over. "And, let's face it, there'll be plenty of birds with nice rooms in boarding houses to stay with." He looked back over to the girls packing who were still giggling and staring, then turned back to his friend, whose ego had now kicked in.

"Well, it's not the worst idea I've heard." He smiled at the girls who suddenly collapsed in gales of laughter. "Let's talk it over with the boys, see what they say".

"Brilliant! Ah, I tell you Billy, it'll be mint!"

"We'll see, lad. We'll see."

Billy returned to his position under the conveyor and placed his spanner on a retaining bolt. Moving his body so that his full weight was behind it, his backside came on full view to James. Chuckling to himself, James checked around and reached under the conveyor, grabbing his friend's backside.

Billy jumped a mile, the spanner turning the bolt loose as he cracked his head on the underside of the belt.

"Arrgh!" He cried, sliding out from under the belt, one hand on his head, the other on his arse.

James was bent double with laughter, tears springing from his eyes.

"You bastard!" cried Billy.

Before James could answer, the alarm started ringing as the bolt Billy had loosened came away, the belt unravelling and thousands of wafer biscuits tumbled to the floor.

"Oh fuck." They said in unison.

Chapter Three
One more sleep until...

Roger was standing at the bar, waiting for the Steward to stop chatting up the new bar maid and come over to serve him.

The music from the resident duo of keyboard and drums thudded away in the background, making it difficult to be heard but the chatter of the club rose above it. The pianist occasionally added little flourishes to the end of each set of notes, causing the drummer to miss his beat on several occasions. Roger knocked on the damp wood of the bar to get the stewards attention.

"Eh, Geoff!" He shouted.

Geoff had his chin on the girl's shoulder and his hand on her waist, his back to the bar.

"What?" He asked, not looking around.

"Can we have some service?" He looked around him and saw Bobby the postman waiting too. A tall, hulking man, with a huge red beard, Roger had known him since school and his wife worked in the factory offices with Maureen.

"Now then Bobby lad" he acknowledged him. "You alright?"

"Grand" replied Bobby. "Be better if I had a chuffing drink though."

"I'll be with you in a second" said Geoff, his hand on the bar maid's backside now, muttering and laughing into her neck. She was forcing a smile, wishing she could be anywhere but there, at that moment.

"Come on!" shouted Bobby, "I was frigging clean shaven when I walked in here tonight".

Geoff turned and faced the men over the bar, Roger chuckling at Bobby.

"What can I get you?"

Smarmy bastard, thought Roger, the bar maid had taken her chance and had scuttled off to collect glasses from the concert room.

"A pint of John's and a gin and orange please" said Roger. Eric took hold of the shiny ceramic beer pump and pulled, his full weight behind it. He was a slightly built man, with slicked back hair and a pencil moustache, like a world war two spiv. In his fifties now, though he wouldn't admit it, he'd done many jobs before landing the Steward's role here. Landed on his feet as well, with a lovely flat above the club, rent free. He said he hailed from Leeds, but no-one knew for sure. He'd avoided National Service on some mystery condition; that's what Roger did know and he wasn't liked for it.

A frothing pint of John Smith's bitter was placed on the bar and next to it, the gin and orange for Maureen. Geoff placed a cocktail cherry in with an umbrella with a flourish and a wink.

"For the lady" he said.

"Thanks" Roger replied unenthusiastically and scooped up his change from the five pound note he'd handed over, pocketed it and took the two glasses from the bar, over to his wife at their table.

The concert room was a grand affair, polished mahogany panelling with ornate red flock wall paper up to the corniced ceiling. A large chandelier hung down from the centre, over the sprung dancefloor, around which, small tables and stools were placed in front of upholstered banquette seating. In one of these was Maureen, who was talking to Mrs Whiting, the next-door neighbour in the seat beside theirs and, judging by their expressions, it was something womanly that they were discussing. Roger put the glasses on the table, smiled at Mrs Whiting, who gave him a cold look in return, to which he sighed, raised his pint to his lips, and took a deep drink of the ice-cold bitter. He put it back on the table and looked around him.

His wife was still talking away to her neighbour but had started on her drink, her mouth chewing away on the cherry.

The room was full, as it usually was on a Saturday night but especially tonight, as everyone was getting ready for factory fortnight, excited at the two weeks break and making sure their plans were in place. Most of the holidays were booked through the club, the affiliation being able to negotiate huge discounts through the companies and the patronage of the brewery.

Roger could see a lot of the factory here, with a few from other trades joining in, alongside those from the Royal Mail sorting office, just over the river, their spouses or parents being connected with the chocolate factory. He noticed a few lads from the Carriage Works, ABB, who made all the rolling stock for British Rail and abroad. They were knocking off for their fortnight too, their management understanding the need for everyone to get away at once. The lads were laughing away over by the bar and Roger could hear the distinctive brogue of Scotland and Tyneside coming over, lads moved down to Yorkshire to work at the main plants.

Roger took another deep drink of his pint and checked the clock. Only fifteen minutes until bingo. Best drink up.

He spotted Dennis over in the corner, talking to the Chairman. His old mate Dennis who he'd been in the army with, both of them in the Lancers, driving tanks. Although Dennis didn't do much driving tanks, on account of being sick. Constantly.

He could see him with his book of raffle tickets and tin of money, chatting away, a Rothman cigarette dangling from the corner of his mouth, bouncing and dropping ash on the carpet as he spoke. He didn't work, only did 'favours' at the club and, over the years, had made himself indispensable, nothing that would jeopardise his benefits.

Roger looked back to his wife, still deep in conversation, so he finished his pint, wiped the froth from his lips and stood up to go back to the bar. He looked at her, received a nod that meant 'yes, I'll have another' and, without a word, he turned to walk away.

"Same again Eric" he said when he got to the bar.

"Having another one?" he heard Dennis' voice next to him. He must have moved with such stealth, he made Roger jump at the sound of his voice. Like a stoat on rails, he moved silently around the bar, waiting for a drink to be bought, never opening his wallet.

"Now then Dennis." Said Roger. Pause. "Pint?"

"Ah, thank you very much" replied Dennis. His rotund body was encased in cheap polyester and his face was a sheen of sweat, his greased fringe falling over one eye. Roger nodded to Eric, who pulled another pint of John Smith's, laid the drinks on the bar and took Roger's pound notes that were laid out on the soggy bar towels.

"You off away then, Dennis?"

"Aye" he slurped his pint, a third gone in one mouthful.
"I'm helping the organising committee with the entertainment"

Roger understood what that meant. Dennis had got himself a free trip for the fortnight, taking up jobs that the other committee members couldn't be arsed with or knew that they'd be too pissed to complete.

"And the wife and bairns?" asked Roger. "Are they looking forward to it?"

"Oh, she'll be busy here" Dennis replied, looking askance.

Roger looked at him, amazed. Dennis took another pull on his pint and looked at Roger.

"Well, with no-one here, it's perfect." He said.

"Perfect for what?" Asked Roger, incredulous.

Dennis nodded his head over towards the dance floor.

"That won't get buffed up on its own."

Over at the edge of the stage, the committee chairman was moving the bingo equipment. Seeing this, Dennis took his queue.

"Best be off! Thanks for the pint." He waddled off towards the stage, leaving Roger with his mouth open.

He took her drink over to the table and began to speak to Maureen,

"I'll be in the back bar…" he began his sentence just as the lights changed in the hall and a heavy silence fell over the concert hall …."so I'll…" he tried to continue

"SHHHH!!" several voices hissed at him, pens poised above bingo cards, the air suddenly thick with excited anticipation.

"Bollocks" he whispered and left the hall, moving out to the back bar, where he saw most of the other men, evacuated as they all were, during the holy state of bingo.

Chapter Four
The Dye is Cast

The evening light was starting to fade as the lads walked down Coney Street, the main road through the centre of town. The shop lights all along were lit and Billy lingered at the window of Leak and Thorpe's, the big department store, and looked at the menswear on display. James ran up beside him and performed a Harry Worth leg-raise at the corner of the window, his legs dancing in mid-air in the reflection of the plate-glass.

Billy, Michael, James, Slim and their old school friend, Nutty were all dressed for a big night out. Pay packets bulging, they all had on their best clothes and were primed to celebrate finishing work for two weeks. They made a mismatched lot, ranging from Slim at only five feet six, up to Nutty at six foot four, his bright red hair like a beacon in the evening light.

Laughing, they moved off again, chatting, dodging the crowds of people moving from pub to pub through the city centre. Different age groups went in different directions and, in the background, the sound of cheering went up as people completed the infamous 'Micklegate Run', fourteen pubs on one road and a drink in each completed the challenge, although it was never remembered.

They came to the corner at St Helen's square and looked around. There were some groups heading down into the Lendal Cellars, an old merchants store next to the river, converted to a pub, whilst some were headed down Stonegate towards the Minster and the pubs surrounding the vast cathedral, but the boys had different ideas.

They turned and went towards Betty's tearooms where they saw the staff cleaning after a busy day of cream teas and tourists. A heavy door was propped open to the right of the café and James led the party down the steps, into the Oak room bar, which sat beneath. Michael and Slim were close behind him, with Billy and Nutty, bringing up the rear.

As they descended downwards, they walked through several layers of cigarette fog that surrounded every table and they had to squint to see the bar and who was in there that night. Nutty had the practically bend double to avoid cracking his head on the door jamb but straightened up as soon as he was in, his red hair catching the light.

Billy strode forward towards the bar, eyes moving left and right, he took in every table and every female in the place without breaking stride.

"My round lads" Out came a fistful of fivers, making sure everyone saw him. Several pairs of eyes swivelled in his direction, mainly the women's with a few of the men looking too, knowing his reputation.

"Five pints of Hoffmeister please" he called to the bartender.

The bar was dimly lit, the lights behind the bar showing the mirrors that had the names of RAF and foreign pilots scratched on them from the war. Billy's own granddad was on there, the only reason his family were in York now. Polish by birth, he'd settled after war, married Billy's grandmother and the rest, they say, is history.

Five foaming pints arrived on the bar where the lads lined up, clinked glasses and said a resounding cheers.

"Right lads, "said James, "this is the last night out before we head to the coast on Monday. So, let's make it a good one."

They were all in their best clothes, tight trousers and patterned shirts, tucked in at the waist. Billy had his half-sovereign medallion nestled in his chest hair, it caught the lights of the bar occasionally, glinting like a beacon of sexuality to all who looked over. And it was most people.

"We shouldn't spend all our money before we go", whimpered Slim. He looked awkward compared to the rest of them, his leather jacket not fitting correctly and his trousers scraping the ground where his mother had taken them up. Badly.

"Ah, shut up Slim." Cried Michael, "the whole point of us going camping is to have money to spend." He stank of brut aftershave and his attempt to look like Billy was marginally good but couldn't quite pull it off. His brother James wasn't much different.

"Aye, would you rather be in some stuffy guest house or out in the fresh air for nowt?" Billy added.

"I know what you're trying to say but…"

"There's always a but with you, lad" Said Michael.

"I'm just saying, we would be better saving our money so that we have more to spend in Brid'."

"The best things in life are free, Slim" replied Billy, catching the eye of a girl on the dance floor.

The room was beginning to fill and the music was starting to take on a disco vibe. Boney M was coming through the speakers loudly and some people were already up and dancing on the small floor at the far end of the room. Billy's attention focussed upon two girls, wearing very tight trousers, moving along to the music. Michael followed his gaze.

"You're not wrong lad" he said, took a long pull on his beer and walked over to the dancefloor, closely followed by Billy and James.

Nutty and Slim were left at the bar, looked at each other and carried on drinking. The room was heavily smoke-filled and people were jostling and nudging to get past to the dance floor or to the bar for refills. Slim felt himself pushed as people squeezed past him, trying not to spill his drink, he looked over at Nutty and tiptoed to try and speak into his ear.

"Mum and Dad aren't happy with me doing this, you know" He shouted at his friend.

"Why not?" Nutty asked him, he looked above his friend at a group of girls that had just walked in, most of whom he recognised from the factory, even though they looked very different in civilian clothes.

"They want me to go to Torremolinos with them."

That got Nutty's attention.

"Where? Torremolinos? Why the bloody hell are you coming with us, then?"

"I dunno", Slim smiled shyly, "I suppose I want to do my own thing you know? Be independent."

"You're frigging daft son." Nutty laughed at him. "A free trip in the sun and you'd rather be in Bridlington with us lot. Crackers."

"No, think about it. I can't be free with me mam and dad watching over me."

"And what will you be free to be do in Brid' that you can't do in Spain?"

"Well," Slim smirked, "Girls and that, y'know?"

Nutty spat beer out as he laughed at that one. As he wiped himself clean, he noticed Slim's look of hurt.

"I'm sorry, mate, I didn't mean to laugh, it's just that…"

"What?"

"Well, you're hardly a Casanova, are you?" Nutty tried to pacify him. "Have you even had a bird?"

Slim looked forlorn at the bar, staring into his pint.

"No" he finally admitted, even though Nutty had known the answer to that question.

"Look," said Nutty, as he placed his glass on the bar, "Your time will come but you have to be patient. You're the kind of guy that, well, that…" He stumbled slightly.

"Yes?" Demanded Slim.

"No, I didn't mean nothing by that." He lied.

Slim looked up at his friend with puppy eyes.

"You did."

"No, I meant that…"

"What?"

Nutty paused, though about what he was going to say for a second, not wanting to hurt his friend anymore and wishing the conversation had never started. His eyes lit up as he thought of something.

"You might find a fat bird in Bridlington!" He said triumphantly and turned his back to the bar to watch his other mates doing their stuff on the dance floor.

Slim looked destroyed but turned to look over all the same. It didn't help. He was envious of them. Long haired, tight trousers and lumps in all the right places, unlike himself. It could be a long evening

Back in the working men's club, the evening's entertainment was about to start.

"Now then, Ladies and Gentlemen" The Chairman's voice boomed through the microphone across the smoky haze in the club concert room. His lips were right against it but it sounded like he was speaking from the urinals next door. "It's time for the end-of-the-night finale. Key to the door and the meat raffle"

Dennis was touting the raffle tickets around each table, strips of tickets laid out next to pints of beer and glasses of Babycham, pointing at the two trays of meat laid out, gleaming under cellophane at the top table, getting hot and slightly sizzling in the concert hall lights.

The Chairman took a bag full of keys, jingling them across the dance floor, looking for a worthy volunteer to pick out the key that would fit the pine-panelled box, containing the latest accumulator amount.

"Now, it's been five weeks since this has been won, so the pot stands at…" he paused for effect, "£20! Which would be handy just before everyone goes off on their holidays"

He looked though the smoke and saw Maureen at her table, her husband Roger trying to talk but she was more interested in the proceedings. By, she looked good, he thought. He'd always fancied her.

"Now then Maureen, love. Would you do me the honour?" He said smarmily into the microphone.

Roger's heckles went straight up. Ever since school, this lad had had the hots for Maureen. Even after their marriage and two kids, he still kept sniffing around.

Maureen smiled and stood, theatrically dipping her hand into the bag.

"Now then Maureen, love" He talked to the crowd, with one hand on the bag, "Give your hand a good rub around, heh" feeling her fingers writhe around inside the bag.

"Oh, you," said Maureen, in mock exasperation.

"Once your hand's in, you never know what you might find."

Roger was nearing apoplexy at the banter with his wife. Maureen moved her hand around, trying to avoid his fingers. She stopped suddenly and looked him in the eye.

"Found it love?" he winked.

Her eyebrows raised as a key was pushed into her hand.

"I think so." She replied gingerly.

Pulling out a key, she raised it up to show the crowd. He lifted her out of her seat slightly as he took her by the elbow and led her to the box. Maureen could feel Roger's eyes boring into her back from their table.

"Drum roll please, Geoff" The Chairman signalled to the drummer on the stage.

As the snare drum rattled, Maureen placed the key in the lock of the box. It turned.

"Hey!" He shouted, dramatically, "Maureen's done it!"

A loud cheer went up from the gathered throng in the concert hall.

For the first time in hours, Roger smiled, £20, he thought; lovely.

Maureen held the envelope aloft to the crowd that cheered her. The Chairman grabbed her elbow.

"I hope you won't forget this Maureen" he whispered in her ear. Roger's smile turned to dust at the sight of this.

She turned and smiled sympathetically at him.

"No, I'll buy you a drink in Brid'."

"More than that, I hope my love?"

Maureen extracted her arm with some force.

"We'll see." she said and made her way back over to Roger. Her every step was followed by his gaze.

"Hmmm" he said to himself. As he watched, he saw Roger's fierce glare firing at him.

"Now! The meat raffle!" He announced. As he turned to the torn-up tickets in the hat, he could feel Roger's eyes boring into him from behind. Time to make amends.

His hand moved within the hat, with a couple moving down from beneath his sleeve. Prepared for any eventuality, he knew how to calm the waters.

"And the winning number is…." He looked around the room, taking in the expectant gazes of all gathered.

"072" He shouted. The room was filled with a shuffling of paper and a resounding hum of disappointment.

Maureen looked at the numbers on the table and looked at Roger. His gaze was fixed firmly on the front of the stage, when she tugged him by the elbow and hissed, "It's you, y'daft sod"

"Me?" He looked at her and then back at the Chairman who was grinning as he surveyed the room. "Really?"

He stood and walked across the floor towards the stage. The Chairman was smiling in an ingratiating manner as he took the ticket off Roger and handed the navvies breakfast and gammon over to him.

"Well done Roger!" He announced into the microphone.

"Thank you." he spoke into it, as it was held to his face. When the Chairman had dropped it to his side, Roger looked at him and whispered: "Go near my wife again, I'll fucking kill you"

Chapter Five
Preparations…

Roger freewheeled his bike along the alley, having called for a paper and cigarettes and drew to a halt by his back gate. He stretched, yawned, still trying to adjust his body to not being on night shifts. The morning was hot again already and the streets were coming to life with a bit more vibrancy as everyone was now off for a full two weeks.

As he opened the back gate, the sight of his lads and their friends bustling about the yard, was an assault on his eyeballs and his tired, addled brain.

Michael and James were laying out a large, canvas tent in the tight confines of the back yard while Billy, Nutty and Slim, were trying to light some burners, with the smell of kerosene strong in his nostrils.

"What the fucking hell…" he stopped short of finishing the sentence as a strong knuckle rap on a bedroom window above, stopped him. Looking up, he could see Mrs Whiting, her face was thunder, pressed against the glass of her sash window. Lip reading skills minimal, he could make out a few swear words from her, as she pointed and grimaced at the carnage and noise that was going on below.

For once in his life, Roger agreed with her. He nodded wearily at her and raised his hand as if to say: 'I know, I'll sort it out'.

"Morning Dad" said James called brightly from somewhere inside the canvas of the tent.

"Morning Mr Brown" Slim and Nutty said together. Billy just grinned at him.

"Please tell me this is not real." Said Roger.

"It is, Mr Brown, we'll not be long and we'll be on our way"
Billy smiled up at him, blowing on his fingers after the
kerosene had taken off his finger prints.

Roger pushed his way past them, looked Billy in the eyes
and muttered, "Get your fucking haircut."

"Will do Mr Brown," called Billy as Roger went into his
kitchen, slamming the door behind him.

"What's up with him?" he asked.

"Fuck knows" said James. "Come on then, let's get this all
packed up."

"We're not ready yet" Slim came out from behind the
kerosene burner, brushing the cinders off his trousers.

"We are ready, what else is there to do?"

"Supplies" He said, "what are we going to eat?"

Billy put a warm arm around him and said, thoughtfully.
"Slim. You'll not starve. We can stop on the way. If we pack
everything now, we'll be pedalling tons up the bloody hills.
Think about it."

"Oh yeah."

"What about drink?" asked Nutty.

"Well, that's a different matter my friend." Michael opened
the shed door with a flourish and revealed four crates of
Skol lager.

All five of them took in the sight before them and nodded in
appreciation.

"Very good," said James.

"And how are we carrying that?" Asked Nutty.

As a man, the rest of them turned to look at the assembled
bikes leant against the alley wall, beyond the door. Nutty
had one of his father's butcher's delivery bikes from the
shop. The steel basket in front would hold many bottles.
Nutty looked at the bike then back at his friends.

"Ah no, come on, lads"

"You are the supply train. Think cowboy. Think sustenance" Billy soothed him, an arm around his shoulder.

A loud bang sounded on the kitchen window behind them. They turned to see Roger there, his fist against the glass.

"Fuck off!" He mouthed through the window.

Michael started rolling the tent quickly.

"Best move lads."

Inside the kitchen, Roger was getting increasingly pissed off with them. His yard was a mess, he had packing to do and where was Maureen? Why weren't they at Slims house, with his Dad's big garden in Heworth? Bloody kids. Maureen came up behind him and looked out at the mayhem.

"What's that?" she asked.

"A tits-up from what I can see" replied Roger and he turned to get his breakfast. "Where have you been? Did you know about this?" He slammed the kettle down on the gas hob and impatiently clicked at the igniter, still looking at his wife.

"Know about what?" She asked, innocently. She watched him for a second. "You're trying to light the wrong hob." Roger looked at what he was doing and tutted before moving the igniter to the gas hob that had been hissing gas for a while. It woomphed into flame, making him jump back.

"Christ Jesus!"

"What are they doing?" Maureen asked, ignoring him.

"Bunch of twats" said Roger.

"No, I asked what they were doing not what they were." She smiled at the sight outside in the yard. "He's a lovely looking lad, that Billy."

"Bollocks". Roger replied, following her gaze. "They'll wreck all of my kit. Didn't even ask!"

"And when did you last use it?'" She asked

"That's not the point" he said, bitterly. "It would've been nice to be asked."

Maureen ignored him and leaned out of the back door.

"Cup of tea, lads?" She called out and received a chorus of approval from them.

"Don't be bloody offering them drinks! I want them gone."

"Gone where? Where are they going?"

"Think about it. No money, time on their hands. They're off to the bloody coast!" He poured hot water into a teapot and slammed the lid back on. "They're going to wreck my holiday with their toss-pot ideas."

"Oh, I think it's a great idea, what an adventure." She reached for some mugs and placed them on a tray. "You did the same when you were their age, went camping all over with Sid, didn't you?"

He looked amazed at his wife and put his teaspoon onto the draining board with a clatter. "That was bloody National Service, Maureen. We didn't get a frigging choice, y'know."

"Come to think of it, isn't that tent from then?" She watched as James finished rolling the canvas tent, clearly showing the 'MOD PROPERTY' legend sprayed on it.

"That's still not the point, and you know it." He slurped his tea aggressively.

"Are you a bit jealous, Rog? They're all off without a care in the world."

"All I'm saying is, I had better things to do with my time when I was that age."

"Like what?" she asked.

"I was married, with James and Michael was on the way"
He lifted a pan onto the hob.
"Oh, I see, tied down too young, is it?"
"You know what I mean."
Maureen looked back out at her sons and his friends, laughing and joking as they loaded their camping gear onto their bikes.
"Well, if you have regrets, say it now." She was leaning against the worktop, with one hand on her hip, ready to launch. Roger swallowed loudly.
"I'm not saying that and you know it. I was just saying…."
"If I hadn't let you get me fucking pregnant, you'd have been off too, is that it?" she shouted.
Outside, the lads had stopped, hearing the raised voices. Looking at each other, they quietly began shuffling kit into the alleyway.
Maureen turned and stormed upstairs, every step reinforced by the heel of her shoes before the bedroom door slammed shut.
Roger sighed. He walked over to the foot of the stairs and put his head against the handrail.
"Maureen, I'm sorry" He called up gently.
"Fuck off!" A muffled shout came back
"I'm just tired after the all the night shifts, I'm sorry." He repeated.
"You heard me."
"Let's not start our holiday on a bad foot." He walked back into the kitchen and picked up his tea cup. Looking outside, he saw that the lads had gone, leaving a trail of devastation in their wake. The back gate rolled open under its own weight and he saw Slim trying to mount his bike, which

was set too high for him. He heard the others laughing at their mate.

"Lucky bastards" he said, suddenly feeling his age.

Chapter Six
Coach trip

George Rivers was busy, his clipboard held in front of him, ticking off every passenger, bag and eventuality that came his way.

It was a bright, early morning, the sun was already giving out a fair amount of heat, lifting the mist from the river which flowed slowly at the bottom of the street. The city walls were still creating shadow, the sun not yet above them, as George waited. Across the city, the chimes of York Minster sounded seven o'clock.

A Pullman's coach was pointing up the hill, its driver tapping the wheel impatiently as he waited to be off. People had been turning up for over an hour, dropping bags and hauling themselves aboard. He had helped for the first thirty minutes, then given up. Sod them, they could put their own bags away.

George was pacing now as they were due to be off and he was still twenty bodies short of the full bus. Why did he do this every year, organise the bloody trips?

Around the corner came a group of girls, silhouetted against the sunlight at the end of the road. Squinting to see who it was, he checked his list and ticked off his girls from the factory enrobing room. Ivy, Brenda, Irene and Beryl were clacking down the hill in their heels, struggling with bulging cases and handbags. George looked into the drivers cab and slapped the side of the bus to get his attention.

"Ey, you, come on, give these lasses a hand."

The driver turned his head slowly, removed the cigarette from his mouth, laconically checked his watch and shook his head.

"Should be driving now, mate. Not lifting."

Tutting, George strode forward and took the first two cases from the girls.

"That lazy bastard won't help" he said, tilting his head at the driver. Through the glass, he saw him mouth the words 'piss off' and smile. George narrowed his eyes back at him. 'Wanker' He mouthed back.

"You're looking lovely girls!" He said to them, as they put their cases in the hold.

They all giggled. After months of working for him, here he was, lifting their bags.

"Nice outfit George!" said Ivy, the oldest one of the gaggle and the most brazen. She and her friends were all in their best clothes, especially bought for their break away from the factory. But then, so was George.

George checked them on board and waited for the next tranche to turn up. He didn't have to wait long.

Around the corner came a loud, raucous shouting as Roger, Maureen and a platoon of regulars from the working men's club strode down the hill, suitcases in hand, the women carrying bags for the coach, loaded with sandwiches and snacks for the journey to Bridlington.

"Come on, then" shouted George, "We need to be off!"

"Coming Petal!" retorted Roger. The rest of his entourage laughed, accompanied as he was by several regulars from the club and fellow workers from the factory. Every one of them was a fifties throw-back with greased quiffs and sideburns, looking uncomfortable in their shirt and ties, dressed as they were by their wives.

"Cheeky fucking bastard," muttered George beneath his breath.

As the blokes walked past the doors to the club, they put down their cases and started hammering on the doors. The noise echoed beyond the street and bounced off the city walls behind them.

"Come on Eric, you toss-pot!" They shouted through the letter box as they were rattling the doors on the hinges. Beyond the door, they could hear footsteps and cursing. Sid stopped hammering and, folding his arms, leant one shoulder against the door, waiting for it to be opened.

"Something tells me he won't be happy at being knocked up" He laughed to Roger when suddenly, the doors opened and Sid tumbled sideways into the lobby, his arms still folded. He hit the doormat with a loud thud.

"Bollocks!" he shouted when he had landed.

Eric was stood there in his dressing gown, bleary eyed and snarling.

"Do you know what fucking time it is?" He shouted. Then he noticed the ladies standing there and immediately apologised.

"I'm sorry ladies, foul language; no excuse."

"That's ok Eric," said Maureen, "we've heard worse."

From the coir matting in the entrance to the club, Sid was struggling to get himself up, brushing dog-ends from his best shirt.

"Where are the crates, Eric?" Roger asked.

Eric looked down at him then back at the assembled throng in front of the club doors.

"Oh, for Christ's sake. Hang on." He walked away into the bar and came back with two crates of pale ale bottles, rattling against him as he huffed and puffed back to the lobby.

"Here you go" he handed them to Sid who had lifted himself from the floor and was being dusted down by his wife, Barbara, who was tutting and muttering about the state of his shirt.

"Thank you, Eric,! We'll see you in a couple of weeks, eh?" Sid lifted the crates against his chest and started moving towards the coach.

"Aye, try not to miss us too much!" said Roger, laughing.

"Send us a postcard" Eric retorted, turned and slammed the doors behind him.

As they all boarded the bus, the sun was just peeking above the City walls and hitting the large windows, creating a greenhouse effect inside. Some of the passengers were fanning themselves with newspapers and magazines, while some were already quenching their thirst with bottles of beer at only 7.30am.

Roger, Maureen, Sid and the rest of them shuffled sideways down the aisle to their seats near the back. Greetings and hellos were called out as they moved through, Sid struggling with the two crates of beer, catching every seat and head of passenger as he went by.

"Sorry, sorry" he repeated.

"Christ, Sid! You nearly took me head off!" One of the girls from the factory cried, as she pushed her hair back into position.

"Sorry, love" He found their seat, plonked the crates on the table and dived into the window seat with a cheer.

George stood at the front of the coach, next to the driver, his clipboard in front of him. The driver started the engine with a diesel roar.

"Eh, not yet!" He shouted at the driver, who promptly shut the engine off, to many boos from the gathered passengers.
"Right, roll call" He shouted at the throng.
Sid promptly stood up to attention and shouted, "24534 Gunner Hodgson, Sir!" To peals of laughter.
"Bugger off Sid" George shouted back.
He went through all of the names, checked everyone was there that should be and then sat in the seat directly behind the driver.
"On you go driver" He tapped the man on the shoulder.
With a sigh and an eye-roll, the driver turned the key in the ignition, to a loud cheer from the passengers, and ground the gear stick into first, pulling up the hill to the main road.
"Yay!" cried Maureen. "At last! We're off!"
Roger popped the lid off one of the beer bottles, handed it to her and smiled.
"Let's go!" He shouted.
The sound of bottles opening was repeated along the bus as everyone began their holiday, the driver was hit suddenly with a whiff of beer as he pulled out into the city centre and made his way out of town and onto the coast road. He was soon behind a convoy of buses, all heading in the same direction.
When he got to the dual carriageway, he saw a chance to pull in front of one of his colleagues in another bus. As they passed, a loud cheer went up from the passengers behind him, while the bus being passed was a forest of two-fingered salutes from the crowd inside, with everyone standing and gesturing at their opposite numbers.
Roger stood and replied with his own salute.
"Fuck off you tossers!" he shouted whilst Sid was laughing his head off with Maureen was grabbing Roger's waistband.

"Shut up you daft sod!" she pulled him back into the seat next to her.

"Ah, come on love, it's just a laugh"

"There's no need for that language" she replied.

"Sorry pet" He said, suitably chastised.

"What you need to do is this!" With a jump, she was up, suddenly followed by Sid's wife, Barbara, who followed her lead.

Before they could stop them, they were up on the table, skirts raised, showing their knickers to the other coach as they slowly took over.

"Yayyyy!" they shouted, to loud cheers from everyone on both their own coach and that of the opposite one. The other coach was nearly leaning over onto its side, as everyone moved to the right, looked and leered.

"For Christ's sake Maureen!" Cried Roger, his head in his hands.

"Fucking hell Barbara!" Sid shouted at his wife.

She turned to look at him.

"Bugger off!" She shouted. "We're on holiday!"

A huge cheer went up from everyone else on the bus, laughing raucously at the antics going on.

George stood up and, holding onto the drivers head rest, he tried to balance himself.

"Right!" he shouted, "Time for a song!" more cheers.

The driver clicked on the radio and the coach was filled with ELO's Mr Blue Sky as the coach roared its way out of the city, with forty voices shouting along, and onto the country roads that led to the coast.

Every little window on every bus that was leaving town, was open, with shouts and laughter pouring out, along with cigarette smoke, leaving a trail of nicotine and diesel fumes in their wake.

Factory fortnight had begun.

Chapter Seven
The Long Road to Bridlington

Slim took a long pull from the bottle of dandelion and burdock that was in the front basket of his mum's bike and drank until the fizz started to hurt his throat. The others were adjusting panniers and sleeping bags on theirs, tightening bungee straps and taking a drink as they chatted. They had got as far as Stamford Bridge, seven miles outside York on the Bridlington Road and they were already knackered.

It was only seven in the morning and refreshingly cool but, at their pace, the sun would hit them hard when it got going. The pubs weren't even open.

They'd pulled over to the side of the road and propped their bikes by the River Derwent, which was flowing sluggishly over the weir, the dry, hot summer taking its toll. A couple of fishermen were already out, taking advantage of the low levels to get the legendary pike that was rumoured to be in it.

The lads were all in tight shorts and t-shirts, just in case they saw any girls on the way there but Slim's shorts were tight by default and reached down to his calves, his attempts to roll them up having lasted only ten minutes of cycling.

Nutty leant down to dip his fingers in the water, watching the tiny bull-head fish dart all over as he did so. He cooled his hands down, a blister already appearing on his left palm from leaning too heavily on the handlebars, his dad's bike being too small for him. He turned and looked back at his friends, who were standing hands on hips, Slim chewing something, and wondered why in God's name had they decided to do this. He strode back to them.

"You're lucky not to lose your arm in that water, lad." James said to him, his forearms resting on his head as he breathed deeply, trying not to throw up after the morning's exercise on top of last night's beer.

"Why?" Nutty asked.

"That monster pike them lads are after." The voice came from below as Michael was laid on the grass verge, chewing a grass stem.

"Bollocks" Said Nutty, walking back to his bike.

"It's true. It's taken Labradors out of the water" James replied.

"Double bollocks" muttered Nutty, to everyone's laughter.

Billy lifted his bike from the railings and positioned it on the edge of the road.

"Right lads, best crack on, eh?"

Michael lifted his head from the grass and looked at him.

"What's the rush?" he asked.

"Well, bearing in mind the hill we have to climb, I think it's better we tackle it now rather than later, when it gets too hot." A collective groan went up.

"And" he added, "The sooner we get to civilisation, the sooner we can have a pint."

A sudden shift occurred at that statement and, within seconds, bikes were lined up, ready to go.

Shakily, they started to pedal, getting their balance right with the added weight of their camping gear and clothes. Leaving the village, they free wheeled down a slight hill as the road opened out into bright countryside, with crops already high in the fields, ready for harvest, the lads looked around themselves, feeling the breeze in their hair and hearing the calls of various birds. They had the road to themselves as they pedalled steadily along, with an occasional shout of encouragement or a joke from one or the other. The only other sound was the buzz of their rubber tyres on tarmac as they went along

Suddenly, the laughter and conversation died as they turned a corner and, before them, stood Garrowby hill. A huge climb of 1:4 loomed above them up to the highest point of the Yorkshire Wolds, so high, the summit lay distant around many bends, as it weaved its way up nearly 800 feet into the sky.

The lads shuffled to a halt in a squeal of brakes and shoes on gravel, open mouthed at the enormity of it.

"Oh fuck" said Billy.

"Jesus wept" cried Michael.

"My arse hurts" moaned Nutty, then he saw what everyone else did. "Pigging Nora!"

"I'm not doing that!" cried Slim, "I'm off home!" He tried to turn his bike around, only to land on top of it on the tarmac. If they'd been anywhere else, it would have been hilarious. As it was, they were too stunned by their situation to be able to do anything.

"You're bloody not," said Billy, "You're getting your fat arse up that bloody hill and we're coming with you. Bloody pushing you if we have to."

"Ah, Billy, come on. We'll kill ourselves doing that." Slim was trying to lift his bike off the floor and keep all of the provisions in the basket.

"No, we won't. We're young and fit." He looked at Slim. "Well, we're young."

Michael took hold of one of the handlebars of Slims bike. "Come on, we'll do it in stages. Bit at a time."

"Come on Slim, we don't leave men behind. Let's do the first bit." James lined his bike next to Slim's and smiled at him. "We'll get up it."

Slowly, they lifted their weights onto the pedals of their bikes, to get some momentum and they moved towards the base of the hill, deceptive as it was with a long incline. They all thumbed the levers of their Sturmey-Archer 3-speed gears and felt the chains slacken as they began their ascent. It wasn't so bad. So far.

Then it hit.

The long incline suddenly turned into what amounted to being at the foot of very steep stairs.

Suddenly, they were all standing on the pedals, forcing the pedals around with their body weight. Lungs burning, hearts pounding, they came around another bend and saw a lay-by. Peeling off like fighter pilots, they turned onto the gritty area, gravity stopping them before brakes were needed. They straddled their bikes and leaned over the handle bars, gasping for breath. Slim's head was practically in his front basket and, when he finally lifted it, his face was bright red.

"Ah Jesus." He gasped, "I'm dying."

"No, no, come on. The sooner we do this, the sooner it's over." Billy called over his shoulder and stood on his pedals to move. He went nowhere.

He tried again. Nothing. He paused for a couple of seconds. "Right!" He called. "We're walking up this bastard"

They all climbed off their bikes and began the long, slow trudge up the hill, pushing and huffing as they went.

The heat was beginning to rise on the tarmac as they pushed their bikes up the long, steep hill. Trying to keep in the shade of the trees by the side of the road as they went, a few cars went past, beeping their horns as they went. The lads responded in a sequence of two-fingered gestures. Sweat was dripping into their eyes, their shirts stuck to their backs as they pushed up the hill that seemed never-ending. Another corner.

To their left appeared a huge crucifix that was implanted on the verge, Jesus looking down on them as they panted on and on. Any other day, a sarcastic comment would have ensued but today, no one could draw breath long enough to utter a word. Slim whispered a Hail Mary as they went past and hoped he wouldn't be crucified by this climb.

Behind them, they heard the loud grind of gears as a large vehicle changed down to get up the hill. As one man, they pulled their bikes into the side of the road and stood back, to avoid the blow-back from the vehicle as it went past. Slowly, a coach came into view.

"Ah shite" said Michael.

It was the coach from the club.

All the people on board had their eyes on them as it went past, a sea of faces, hilarity mixed with concern as it went past in what seemed to be slow motion. A few knocks on the windows at the lads, Billy cursing as he saw the girls from the enrobing room pointing and laughing at him.

In the reflection from the polished panels and chrome of the coach as it went by, they could see themselves, a rag-tag bunch of sweaty individuals, red-faced and blowing hard.

"Bollocks" he said. He had high hopes for those girls.

As the coach passed them, out of the back window, Michael and James could see the faces of their parents; their Dad pissing himself laughing and, the last thing they saw, as it went over the brow of the hill, was Maureen, a worried look on her face, her mouth open in a dramatic 'O'.

"Well" said James, "That's cheered the old man up."

"Come on" said Billy, "We're nearly at the top."

Off they went again, the top of the hill in sight now.

"We'll never live that down" muttered Michael.

"We won't live at all, if this hill goes on much longer" huffed Nutty.

The top of the Wolds came into view and the group were greeted by the dramatic scenery of rippling fields full of crops and, behind them, the basin of the Vale of York stretching out behind them. It was a clear day and the Minsters of York and Selby could be seen, along with the new power station, Drax, which punctuated the skyline. Pulling into the side again, the lads pushed their bikes into the verge and collapsed onto the long grass, spread eagled and breathing hard. For a while, no-one said anything, they just concentrated on filling their lungs with air and swilling water around their mouths.

"Christ, I'm knackered." Said Billy. He tried to lift his head, groaned and let it fall back into the grass.

"How far have we come?" Slim asked, his face almost purple from exertion.

"About twelve miles" muttered Michael.

"Is that all?" Asked Nutty, "Jesus, we've thirty to go!" A collective groan went up from the rest of them.

"It's flat from here on though." Said Billy. He lifted his head again to look at the others. "Well, almost." He added.

"Great" said James. "Can't wait."

"Let's take a break, eh lads?" Michael said, lifting himself onto one elbow. "We don't have to kill ourselves getting there, do we?"

"No" muttered James, "we've done that already. This is a staging post for heaven."

With a monumental effort, Slim lifted himself off the grass verge and stood up, adjusting his shorts.

"Where are you off to?" asked James.

"I'm off for a shit." He replied, looking around for somewhere private to go. "All that biking has shifted things. I'm touching cloth."

"Oh, lovely. What a nice image I now have" Mick laughed.

"Piss off" Said Slim, as he stepped over the long grass with some difficulty.

The rest of them watched him skirt the edge of the hedge line until he disappeared into the bushes. He reappeared briefly, tearing up some dock-leaves, then disappeared again.

"I pity the wildlife, me" said Billy, to no-one in particular.

Nutty had also stood up and was stretching out each of his legs, in turn, grimacing. He shuffled his shorts around, adjusting himself and then turned to James.

"Eh, I've got terrible ring-sting, me" he said, grasping his buttocks.

"I'm not surprised with that bloody bike. Where did you get it from?" Asked Billy, also standing up to stretch.

"Me Dad"

"How long has he been in the circus?" asked Michael. The rest of them laughed at him.

"Ha bloody ha. No, seriously, this is sore." He started flapping his backside around, in an attempt to cool the sore area.

"If you go in Slim's basket, he's got some Vaseline. His Mam sent him with everything" Billy pointed over to the woman's bike resting in the hedge, the basket overflowing with kit, sent with love by his mother.

Nutty walked over and started rummaging around.

"He won't bloody starve, I'll say that much for him" Nutty said, picking packets of biscuits up and showing them to the others. "Here it is." He lifted out a large tub of Vaseline. Taking off the lid, he dipped his fingers in, scooping a dollop up and then with his other hand, undid the top button of his shorts. Down went the Vaseline, into the back of his shorts. Nutty started making comforting 'ooh' noises.

"You're not enjoying that are you?" asked James.

"Bugger off" Said Nutty, putting his hand back in the pot for another dollop.

Finishing, he pulled his hand out from the back of his shorts and wiped his fingers on the edge of the Vaseline pot.

"That's better." He said, putting the pot back in the basket of the bike.

"Fully lubricated?"

"Absolutely" Nutty wandered back over to the others, squatted on his haunches a couple of times and smiled. "Amazing stuff, that."

At that point, Slim came back adjusting his shorts.

"Better now?" Asked Michael.

"Yeah, loads better." He said, smiling at them. "I tell you what though, I think I've caught the sun a bit." He patted his face, still red from the morning's exertion and rubbed his lips.

"Right," called Billy, "Shall we move on? It would be good to get there before it gets dark in nine hours."

They all lifted their bikes out of the hedge and moved them onto the road. Slim was still rubbing his lips.

"Hang on" he said, as he reached into his basket and took out the Vaseline tub. Off came the lid and he dipped in his finger.

"No, wait!" Called James.

Pausing, Slim turned to the others, the translucent jelly balanced on the end of his finger.

"What?"

"Oh, nothing" James said, "Sorry. Carry on."

Four pairs of eyes watched as Slim rubbed the jelly into his lips, before rubbing them together and making a smacking noise with them.

"Right, are we off then?" Slim asked. He turned and saw the others, jaws clenched and lips pursed trying not to laugh. Nutty's face was puffed out, trying to stifle a laugh, as snot started to dribble down his top lip.

Billy cracked first, he couldn't hold in the laughter any longer, followed by the others. James fell back into the verge, tears streaming down his cheeks as Michael and Nutty bent double, cackling loudly. Slim looked at them dumbfounded.

"What?"

Chapter Eight
The Road to Shangri-La Part I

The coach noisily changed gears and pulled into the layby next the Black Swan pub in Wetwang village.

George hauled himself up from his seat behind the driver and turned to face the group.

"Half-way house!" He called

A loud cheer went up from the already well-oiled passengers, as handbags and jackets were grabbed and a scrabble started for the doors.

"One at a time!" George shouted, "There's enough for everyone" His voice was lost beneath the footfall and shouts as everyone streamed past him, in a rush to get to the bar first.

He turned to the driver who had switched off the engine and lit a cigarette. He puffed a cloud of smoke out towards George.

"One hour, mate" he said, flatly.

"Alright, I'll have them back." George turned and began to descend the steep coach steps.

"Miserable bastard" he muttered beneath his breath.

"I heard that" the driver called after him.

George walked to the pub and opened the doors, behind the melee, eager to get at the bar.

A mock Tudor building, with low, dark beams and horse brasses greeted them, the floral carpet was threadbare in places, the plush seats past their best. Heavy wrought iron tables with hammered copper-effect tops reflected what light got through the heavy velvet curtains and the half-etched windows were slightly yellowed with nicotine.

The staff looked bewildered at the sudden onslaught and were quickly over-run, pints flowing into glasses and the landlord pulling bitter with all his might. A forest of arms were hanging over into his space, each one holding a collection of pound notes and fivers, shouting orders at the harassed staff, who were running around, reaching up to optics with one hand, the other on the lager taps. The till started ringing at which, the landlord allowed himself a wry smile. Factory fortnight, he thought.

The girls from the enrobing room were shovelling coins into the juke box and laughing as they ran their fingers down the lists. Suddenly, the air filled with the beat of music and John Travolta's voice came over the speakers.

"I got chills…. that are multiplying" he sang. The girls started dancing, whilst still clutching their Babychams.

In the corner of the bar, an old fella watched on. Five minutes ago, he had been nursing his pint in a quiet village pub, now he was watching what looked like Pam's People dancing away next to the juke box. On the one hand, he was annoyed his peace had been shattered, on the other, he was enjoying the show from the young girls in the corner.

Despite himself, he started tapping the table along with the beat of the music. He'd not seen anything like it since VE day.

The bar was starting to clear as everyone gravitated away with their drinks, the landlord and staff breathing a sigh of relief. The Landlord turned and looked at the till drawer, stuffed with notes and smiled again.

The noise and laughter rose and fell, interspersed with laughter, people moved around chatting to different tables and the glasses soon emptied.

George clapped his hands loudly and the noise ebbed enough for him to make an announcement.

"We have to be back on the bus in fifteen minutes!" He called. At which statement, glasses were quickly drained and people started to make their way back to the bar.

The landlord, a Korean veteran, realised the second wave was coming.

"Brace yourselves." He muttered to the staff.

It hit. Notes were fluttering over the bar and orders were called. The girls at the jukebox took possession of more drinks as 'Disco Inferno' came on, by the Trammps. They never missed a beat in the transition and the old fella in the corner was having the time of his life, watching the revealing clothes and young flesh bounce around to the music.

George kept checking his watch as his group necked their drinks. Tutting to himself, he started moving people along, with a 'hurry up' and a 'got-to-get-going'.

Outside, the driver checked his watch too and started the engine. He slid open his window and threw out his fag-end. With a sigh, he pressed the horn for a good five seconds.

Inside, George heard and started physically lifting people out of their chairs, pushing them towards the exit, still with their drinks in their hands.

"Come on, come on. He'll be off without us. I don't trust him"

People started gulping down beer, one arm outstretched holding a pint glass, the other being pulled by George.

He called over to the girls by the juke box.

"You lot!" He yelled, "Get on the bloody bus" Babycham went down in one and the girls made their unsteady way out of the pub.

Pushed out into the bright sunshine from the darkness of the pub, the group stood blinking trying to adjust to the sun.

The bus driver hit the horn again, even as the crowd spilled from the pub.

"Alright, alright" shouted George. "We're bloody coming" He was supporting people's elbows, who in turn, were supporting others, the ramshackle parade unsteadily making its way onto the bus. Leverage was required both at ground level and at the top of the stairs, missed steps and stumbling adding to a cacophony of noise.

"Come on" Muttered the driver.

"Eh!" George said, spinning to face him, "if you were hoping for a tip at the end of this, you've shit-it pal!"

At that, the driver pushed the bus into gear and let the clutch go roughly, lurching the bus forward, sending several people sliding down the aisle on their back-sides, George fell into his seat, cursing.

"I'll not forget this!" He shouted. As the bus moved back onto the road, the singing started again, followed by the 'pop-hiss' of bottles being opened and laughter.

Gears crunching, the bus began to speed up and continue on its journey, the driver quietly praying that no-one was sick before he got to Bridlington, George secretly hoping everyone was, so the driver would have a clean-up job on his hands.

Chapter Nine
The Road to Shangri-La Part II

The bicycle gang were strung-out along the road, panting, sweating and cursing as they pedalled in a semblance of rhythm, the fitter at the front, the unfit bringing up the rear. Every so often, Billy, in the lead, turned his head to look at the pack behind him. He'd never seen a face the colour of Slim's before but, as he hadn't died so far, he thought he might just make it.

They'd made it as far as Burton Agnes village, which was not far from the finish line, when Billy spotted the hanging sign of The Blue Bell Inn as they turned the corner.

"Pit-stop!" He called out to the others, James and Michael were panting heavily behind him, followed by Nutty and, further down the road, Slim soldiered on, his pace quickening slightly at the thought of a pint.

Leaning his bike against the pub wall, Billy stretched out his back with a groan as the others piled up alongside him.

"Jesus, you stink" he said as Nutty pulled up. His shirt was more sweat patch than cloth and the seat of his pants were suspiciously stained by the Vaseline he'd put down there earlier.

"Oh yes? And you smell of roses, do you?" He climbed off the bike, his change in position causing him to grimace with a sharp intake of breath.

"They won't let us in this pub like this" Michael sniffed under his arm pit as he spoke, pulling a face at his own smell.

"Come on Slim!" Called Billy.

"Coming!" He huffed. He pulled up alongside the others and let his bike fall against the wall.

"Your round." Billy made it sound like a statement.

"Eh?" Slim looked up from where he was leaning on his knees to get his breath.

"Last one in, buys the drinks!"

"Since when?"

"Since now. Away you go" Billy turned away, "to the beer garden lads"

Slim sighed and walked around to the front of the pub, a typical, white-washed building on the main road, it had its fair share of people inside, all on their way to the coast. As he stepped inside, he paused to adjust his eyes to the dark interior before making his way towards the polished brass on the bar.

The barmaid was watching him approach the bar like he was a vagrant, her nose turned up in distaste before he'd even spoken to her.

"Five pints of lager, love, please?" He asked, leaning heavily on the bar.

"We are quite busy" she stated, looking at him like a disease.

Slim looked around and saw empty seats. The place was buzzing but hardly packed, then he realised her concern.

"Don't worry love, we've been cycling from York. We'll sit outside."

"Oh," she said, "that's alright then" She began filling the glasses.

"And five bags of crisps as well"

She pulled a battered tin tray from under the bar and began loading the pints on it.

"What flavour?" She asked.

He half-heartedly looked at the piled boxes of Tudor crisps behind the bar and waved his hand at her.

"You choose." He said. He couldn't care less.

She piled the bags up around the glasses, balancing them and tucking them in so he could carry it all.

"That'll be 85p, please."

Slim reached into his shorts pocket and pulled out a few crumpled pound notes, slightly damp from his exertions and handed them to the barmaid. She took them gingerly by the corners, only her fingernails touching them.

"Thank you, love" Slim lifted the tray from the bar and went back outside and around the corner, into the beer garden. The other lads were sitting in the garden, stretched out on the lawn.

The seats around were taken by kids who had been left there by their parents, sipping squash and munching crisps, waiting for mum and dad to come and collect them. A few of the cars in the car park still had kids in the back seat, panting in the heat, wishing they had parents who would stretch to some fizzy pop for them to drink, instead of leaving them stuck to the hot vinyl of the Morris Marina's and Austin Allegro's that were lined up. One kid had managed to slide open a window on a Morris Minor and was half hanging out onto the tarmac, trying to cool down.

Slim laid the tray into the garden wall, each glass with beads of condensation running down the outside as the cold beer felt the heat of the sun. They watched them trickle before they grabbed the glasses greedily. The pints reduced considerably before anyone spoke.

"Thanks, Slim" Said Nutty.

"Lovely" breathed Michael.

"Crisps?" Slim asked, holding the bags out. They were snatched in an instant.

The gammon and pineapple flavour ones were soon thrown back on the tray.

"I'll have them" Slim said.

As they supped their pints and munched crisps, they stayed quiet listening to the children in the beer garden, hot and fractious already, bored of waiting for their parents to finish inside.

"We're nearly there, you know" Billy said, speaking through a mouthful of crisps.

"How much further?" Nutty asked.

"Only about six miles now."

"Fantastic" James said.

"So, we'll get there about three?" Asked Slim.

"We will, then its' tents up, quick wash and out on the town" He rubbed his hands together at the thought of it.

"Thank God" James finished his pint and stood up to stretch his legs. "Come on then, sooner there, the better."

Michael stood up too, followed by Nutty and Billy. The thought of clean clothes and a night on the town had spurred them on.

They went for their bikes, leaving Slim still sitting on the grass who looked at them mounting up, getting ready to leave. He lifted the crisp packet up to his mouth and funnelled in what was left inside.

"I'm ready!" He lifted himself up and waddled over to the others.

A chorus of groans sounded as they mounted the bikes and began pedalling again, stiff joints and aching body parts struggling to find a comfortable position. One by one, they moved away from the pub and into the traffic that was heavier now, making its way through the Wolds villages, towards the coast.

Chapter Ten
Bridlington – Ahoy!

The club bus nudged its way along Marine Drive in Bridlington, behind a convoy of other buses, all filled with factory workers, well-oiled and ready for more.

The air was thick with diesel fumes and cigarette smoke, every window on the coaches opened to help with the heat of the July day but only letting out smoke. Occasionally, the smell of hot chips and vinegar would pervade everything else, and people's noses would lift, smelling the air in anticipation,

Roger took a deep lung full and breathed out, smiling to himself.

"Fresh sea-air, that" he said to the others, all of them puffing away on a shared pack of Rothman's that sat in the middle of the table.

As the coach pulled into the bus station, all of the passengers started to collect belongings, putting playing cards into packs and picking up coats from the racks above. George stood at the front of the bus and tried to call out above the babble of noise.

"I've got your bookings here!" He yelled, "Make sure you pick up your sheet before you head off."

Pages were taken from his hand as people scrambled off the bus, some of them unsteady on their feet. The driver had opened the luggage store and began dragging the cases off but hands reached in around him, so he gave up and let them take what they wanted. He really couldn't be arsed.

As the cases were collected, George shouted one more time.

"Get yourselves settled and we'll meet at the Victoria Sailors Club at 7 o'clock."

He was shouting at retreating backs now, as the busload stumbled away under the weight of their cases and bags, off in various directions to their boarding houses.

"It was a pleasure!" Called George, on his own now. His case was by his feet and the driver had already started the engine, floored the accelerator, and left him in a cloud of fumes.

"Oh, and thank you!" he shouted after the bus.

Straightening his jacket, he picked up his bag and walked off behind some of the others muttering to himself and swearing that this was the last year he would be organiser. Again.

Roger, Maureen, Sidney and Barbara turned a corner into Clarence Road and saw the guest house that they had stayed in every year for the last fifteen years, without fail. The white-washed Victorian terrace had hardly changed in all of that time, its hanging baskets cascading down, framing the large front door with multi-coloured blooms of petunias and sweet peas.

The 'No Vacancies' sign in the window was ready for the onslaught, as all of the other boarding houses were for the summer, booked out months and even years in advance. The windows gleamed in the bright July sunlight and every piece of brass on the door sparkled, not a speck of dust in sight. The doorstep freshly scrubbed; the group smiled as they approached the door. It was a home-from-home for all of them.

Before they could put a finger on the door bell, Mrs Travis, their landlady, was ready and waiting for them.

"Hello, you lot." She smiled at them brightly, her faultless perm and dress was augmented by the ubiquitous pinny she always wore, her fingers adorned with heavy gold rings and stones. She was only five feet four but was a force of nature, having been a landlady for years and running pubs before the guest house, she never took any nonsense. Her voice was gravelly from smoking but she could charm anyone.

"Hello Mrs Travis," said Roger, "you're looking well".

"I can't complain Mr Brown." She stepped aside and let them through. Her husband stood behind her, ready to help with the bags, a stooped man who reached forward and took the bags off the ladies.

"This bugger can though." She said, nodding at her husband. "Come on you, get them bags upstairs."

"Yes love." He mumbled back at her, smiling at the women and not looking at his wife. His eyes wandered over them, from head to toe, stopping at their chests. "Let's go then, ladies."

Maureen and Shirley shoved each other to be the first up the stairs behind him, as he led them to their rooms.

Mrs Travis turned to the men and put the register before them, holding out a pen to Roger.

"The boys not with you this year, love?"

"No, they're doing their own thing this year." Roger scribbled their names in the book, handed back the pen, then reached into his jacket for his wallet. Taking out some crisp ten-pound notes, he handed them over to Mrs Travis, Sid following suit.

"Lovely" she said, her eyes flying over the notes, counting them in a split second. "I'll be serving dinner at six."

With that, she was gone, back into the dining room from which, a lovely smell was emanating. Roger and Sid looked at each other and then heard the women talking loudly upstairs, refusing to be alone with Mr Travis for a second, they were going in and out of each other's rooms.

"Come on", said Sid, "let's get sorted and then hit the town."

The rooms were large, with high ceilings and ornate cornicing matching the furniture that gleamed and smelt of polish. The couple's rooms were opposite each other, only separated by a narrow corridor that led to the shared bathroom at the end. Roger lifted the case onto the bed and unclipped the catches before Maureen shooed him out of the way, not wanting him to mess up her packing.

"Go and see what Sid is up to while I sort this out."

He stepped out of the corridor, only to find Sid standing idly by while Barbara was unpacking. They met each other's gaze and tutted.

"We'll be downstairs love." Called Roger as he and Sid went down to sit in the lounge for a smoke until the girls were ready.

In the lounge, the heavy chintz furniture was immaculate, with lace covers over every chair-back and arm. Roger was slightly daunted to sit down but followed Sid to the high sofa that faced the bay window. Lighting up, Mrs Travis appeared like a flash, reaching for two heavy, leaded ashtrays, which were put lovingly down on lace doyleys on top of the polished coffee table.

"Your wives unpacking then?" She asked, wiping the already gleaming ashtrays out with a duster.

"Aye, we know when to be out of the way." Sid smiled at her, putting out the flame of his match with a quick flick of his wrist, before dropping it with a satisfying chink into the ashtray. He puffed on his cigarette as behind Mrs Travis, they watched others walking up the street, dragging heavy cases, looking for their digs.

A few they recognised from the clubs and pubs of York and they smiled, comfortable in their seats, the bay windows open, sending in a welcome breath of sea breeze.

Mr Travis walked in with a tea towel over his arm, his glasses steamed up, trying to see his wife.

"What do you want?" She barked at him.

"Suet sponge is in, my love." He took off his glasses and wiped them on the tea towel, before sliding them back onto his greasy head. "What next?"

"Give them glasses a polish and finish laying the tables." She turned to look at her two guests on the sofa. "It never stops, you know, I'm worn out!" She stood, checked her hair and face in the mirror above the mantelpiece and turned to her husband, who was still standing in the doorway. "Go on! Shift yourself!" She barked impatiently. She ushered him out, muttering at him, the words 'idle' could be heard as the lounge door closed and the kitchen door opened.

"Poor bastard." Said Roger, who stretched his legs out and sighed with contentment.

"Roger! Sid!" A call came down the stairs and the two men hurriedly put out their cigarettes and jumped up to go upstairs.

Chapter Eleven
On the Beach

The lads pedalled slowly along the last hundred yards towards the gates of South Cliff Camp site, looking in amazement at the packed rows of tents and caravans lined up facing towards the sea.

The place was full of kids and dogs, shouting and screaming, with washing strung up on temporary lines between each plot. The path down to South beach was like a refugee convoy, people carrying bags, balls and wind-breaks up and down the path, eating chips or ice creams, with seagulls circling overhead watching for every dropped morsel.

They all pulled their brakes as one and stopped to look at each other.

"Oh, my good God" breathed Slim.

"You have got to be joking." Michael said to Billy, who was looking speechless.

"It might not be that bad?" Said Billy, after a while.

"Not too bad?"

"Come on. It'll be fine once we're sorted." replied Billy.

"My Grandad was at Dunkirk. He said it was like this." Muttered Nutty

"Shut up."

Billy looked exasperated; they were all staring at him.

"But we're booked in" He said, weakly.

"I couldn't give a shit" James said. "I'm not staying here. Look at it. It's all kids and pensioners; no birds."

"The birds'll be in town though" Billy replied.

"And then what? We bring them back here?" Michael asked.

Billy thought about that for a minute, realising the situation that they were in.

"That's very true" he said, quietly, ruminating on their situation. He then turned to look at them. "So where do we go from here? We can't afford digs."

They all looked at one another.

"Beach." Michael stated.

"What?" Asked the others.

"Beach." He stated again, turning to look at them. "It's big and it's free."

They thought for a minute and began to smile.

"If we head down to the dunes, it'll be private too. No one around."

"We can bring birds back then?" Asked Slim

"We?" Asked Michael.

"Come on," said Billy, "Let's go."

They turned their bike around and headed down towards Wilsthorpe beach, a few hundred yards away.

"You see, this way, we can do our own thing and please ourselves. No rules or regulations." Said James as they pedalled along the road towards the beach.

"And no old rat-bags moaning if we make too much noise." Billy shouted, leading from the front.

As they came out of the streets, they were greeted by long tussocks of grass blowing in the breeze, sitting on top of dunes, which in turn, gave way to clear golden sands, gently sloping down to the North Sea. Waves were gently breaking with the occasional dog-walker throwing sticks into the water but the bulk of the holiday makers were further up the beach, towards south bay, making them appear like a mirage, the heat making them shimmer with sand being dusted upwards from running feet, obscuring them from view.

"This is perfect." Said Billy.

They wheeled their bikes through the deep sand and tucked them between two dunes, out of sight of passers-by, either from the road behind them, or from the beach. Long grass rustled in the wind, adding to their seclusion and the view down to the water was quiet, dotted with a few holiday makers and locals, out walking in the late afternoon sun.

"If we stick the tent up here, no-one will see us." James said as he laid his bike in the sand, letting the panniers dig deep under their weight.

He began kicking the sand over, levelling it, making sure there was nothing hidden beneath. It was fine, soft sand but reached down into thicker, denser stuff that was slightly clay-like, perfect for tent pegs. The others helped and, when a patch big enough to site the tent had been cleared, they scrambled up the small incline of the dune and stood amongst the grasses and looked out, the sea breeze ruffling their long hair.

Slim smiled at the view and turned to look at the bikes that were laid in the sand, laden with their kit.

"Shall we do tent first then?" He asked. Behind him, the others had already begun sprinting down the other side of the dune, towards the sea. Slim turned at the first yelp and watched them kicking sand up in the air behind them, removing plimsolls and t-shirts as they ran. He sighed, then turned and jumped down the dune, whooping as he followed their lead, his short legs digging deep into the soft sand.

Crashing into the water, they began splashing each other, laughing and shouting, cooling off after the long bike ride, not caring about their sweat-soaked clothes that marked a trail into the sea.

They'd made it.

Chapter Twelve
Big Night Out

Roger was trying to shave in the tiny mirror above the sink in the corner of their room. Behind him, Maureen was in her dressing gown, hanging up clothes and laying them out on the bed reverently, trying to decide what she would wear tonight. The room was warm, despite the window being open. Two small chairs were placed around a small card table, covered in a crocheted cloth, a table lamp in the middle.

The room was spotless, its flowered wallpaper matching the swirl of the carpet beneath their feet, deep shag pile under foot adding a sense of luxury. The curtains were heavily lined and perfectly draped across the sash window, the net curtains behind them so white they were nearly blue in the light of evening.

They both heard a knock at the door, Roger turned and opened it a crack; it was Sid.

"Bathroom's free" he announced.

Maureen grabbed her wash bag and followed Sid out into the corridor.

"Won't be long love." She said to Roger, who, in acknowledging her, just nicked himself beneath his nose.

"Bollocks!" he swore.

He rinsed his face and towelled himself dry, splashed some Brut on his face and hissed at the pain from the cut, then put on a clean shirt. Now it would be a waiting game for his wife.

A half-hour later, they were, as a foursome, making their way to the Victoria Sailors Club, a short walk from where they were staying. Roger and Sid in front, the women walking behind and chatting. Both Roger and Sid were smoking as they walked in silence toward the club, looking in at all of the guest house windows and doorways, trying to see if they knew anyone as they made their way to the rendezvous.

As they got closer to the club, they could hear the hub-bub of chatter as other groups of holiday makers were arriving. They turned the corner and the familiar faces of the factory were there, making their way through the doormen and signing into the club's visitor's book.

Alongside the queue, the Bridlington regulars were streaming through to get their usual spots inside. Roger recognised a few faces from years past, the majority of them working at Sara Lee's cake factory, on the edge of the town. Nods and smiles were given, a few shouted hellos and the queue began to dwindle, everyone getting inside to begin the first night of their holidays. Whispers and words were passed down the line, who the 'turn' would be that night and what the jackpot was on the bingo.

Soon enough, they were inside, the women shuffling along banquette seats, banging thighs and knees on the solid cast-iron tables and shouting orders to the men who had sought the bar first, whilst they claimed their seats in the melee. Bags were thrown like shot-puts, taking out seats from general use and cardigans laid across chairs to denote property rights to anyone else.

It was like an aggressive musical chairs, but smiles remained on the faces of the holiday makers, despite some grumbling from regulars.

Roger and Sid turned from the bar, drinks in hands and fags in mouth and looked to where their wives were staking their claim. They both, in an instant, recognised the pursed lips and creased brows of women who weren't to be messed with, twenty years of factory life had hardened them to flint in a, who-belonged-where, in any given pecking order.

Roger looked at Sid.

"Ready?" He asked.

"Ready." Sid responded and they stepped around tables and chairs, lifting their drinks to avoid spillage, as people were rushing to get a good spot in front of the stage.

The room was a large square, with seating around every wall, covered in a red velvet, worn shiny by years of backsides and shoulders, solid tables stood before these, with café chairs lined up, doubling the capacity and all seats pointing toward the stage area. The curtains were drawn, even though it was still bright sunshine outside, creating an air of theatre with the buzz of a crowd, expectantly waiting for the entertainment to start. The fog of cigarette smoke rose and settled, sometimes hitting the wobbling ceiling fans, which merely pushed wisps of the blue smoke back down.

"Who's on, did you see?" Maureen leant into Barbara, shouting into her ear over the noise in the room.

"A comic and a singer" She shouted back. "But it's a toss-up which one will be funnier!"

They were comfortable on the banquette seat, their handbags tucked neatly into their sides, whilst Roger and Sid were perched uncomfortably on the dining chairs in front of the table. Pints balanced, they were poised ready to move should the bingo start or the turn was particularly crap. The bustle of the place was deafening, they could see some of the others from their bus looking around, trying to find seats until they heard George shout up.

"Ooh-ee! Over here!" He was standing on a chair, waving a hanky at the girls from the enrobing room, a large table reserved, which he had been defending for nearly half an hour.

Roger looked over and nudged Sid in the side. Together they watched the young flesh from the factory, all dolled up in short skirts and thigh-high boots, make up freshly applied like war-paint, saunter down the main aisle of the club to the table that George had reserved for them at the front. Roger and Sid's eyes weren't the only ones following the girls. They smiled at each other, then turned back to their wives, who had witnessed the whole thing. Faces set and lips thinned, they stared their husbands out.

Roger turned to Sid.

"Fancy a game of pool Sid?"

"Aye, right." They moved quickly away from their wives and hurried to the bar.

Maureen and Barbara began talking once the men had gone and were only interrupted by the piercing sound of feedback from the club's microphone, followed by the 'tap-tapping' on it, as the club's chairman checked it was on, then cleared his throat loudly, causing everyone to grimace and turn to face the stage.

"Now then, now then." He announced. A rotund man in a badly-fitting polyester suit, his bald head shining through a comb-over under the stage lights, he was enjoying the attention from the crowd.

"First of all," he continued, knowing he had everyone's attention, "I'd like to welcome all our holiday-makers," a chorus of cheers and whistles went up, "and hope you have a smashing time in Brid'." More cheers. "First cab off the rank tonight, is Malc Costello, comedian." He paused for effect. "Then we'll break for bingo" cheers went up from a chorus of female voices. "Then we'll have our summer resident singer for this year…… Micky McDonald!" A resounding cheer went up.

Maureen went as white as a sheet.

"Oh shit" She breathed. Barbara turned to look at her, the smile fading on her lips as she saw the look on Maureen's face.

"What is it?" she asked.

Maureen just swallowed hard, drained her glass in one and shook her head.

In the bar, Roger and Sid were talking as the announcement went out.

"Where have I heard that name before?" interrupted Roger.

"Who? The turn?" Asked Sid.

"It'll come to me." Roger started ruminating while Sid carried on talking about rugby league, how Hull dominated, leaving York behind, when suddenly, Roger slammed his pint on the bar and stood up straight, his eyes wide, beer dripping down his fingers where it had sloshed out of the glass. Sid stopped talking and began staring at his mate.

"What is it Rog?"

"The bastard" He breathed. He wasn't blinking.

"Who?"

"Mickey fucking McDonald" Roger's fists were clenched, knuckles white.

"The turn? Why?" Sid moved his head left and right, trying to see what Roger was staring at and also looking at his friend. He'd never seen him like this.

Roger just carried on staring at the doors to the lounge bar, watching the announcer and saying nothing, just slowly shaking his head.

"Do you not remember? Back in '58?"

Sid raised his eyes in his head, trying to remember, repeating the name in his head, mouthing the words but not speaking. Suddenly, the light came on in his brain.

"You mean that tall Geordie prick? The sparky from the factory?"

"Him. I mean him."

Back on stage, the announcer called on the comedian and, to applause, on strode Malc Costello in sequined jacket and bow tie, sweating under the concert hall lights as he moved his twenty-stone frame to take the microphone. A silence fell over the hall.

"Now then! Welcome to Brid'!" He called out, his voice like marbles in a sock as he pulled the cable around him, microphone and cigarette in one hand, his other gesticulating at the crowd, pointing out a few he knew.

"When did you get out of Armley jail? Heh heh, good to see you."

Barbara was staring at her friend whose colour hadn't yet come back to her face so Barbara poured some of her drink into Maureen's glass, who quickly knocked it back and nearly dropped the glass on the table.

"What is it, Maureen?" Hissed Barbara.

"Shhh!" several voices hushed her quickly. Maureen continued staring ahead.

"Now, I wouldn't say my wife is ugly, but..." The comedian carried on.

Chapter Thirteen
Lock up Your Daughters

The lads had managed to pitch the tent, with much swearing and abuse of each other and had finally got ready to go out on the town. Shirts had been thoroughly shaken to remove creases and a quick dip in the sea had freshened up sweaty bodies. Empty cans were strewn around the site, a mixture of beans and beer and a small stove was still hissing as a stuttering blue flame boiled away water that had been for someone's shave.

Billy tucked his shirt into his waist band, zipped up his very tight trousers, adjusted himself and turned to look at the others. Slim was struggling into his new shirt, the buttons gaping slightly across his belly and the hems of his cords were catching in the sand as he moved around.

"We ready?" Billy asked.

Michael and James were brushing themselves down and Nutty was trying to put his hair in order. And failing.

"Aye" Michael Said, "Ready to go."

"Are we taking the bikes?" Asked Nutty.

"Oh yes, that'll look good won't it? Pedalling into town." Billy replied. "Maybe offer the birds a lift back?"

"It's not far to walk" Michael said." twenty minutes, we'll be in town."

"Walk?" Asked Slim.

"One foot in front of the other. Yes. Walk." James stated.

"I'm knackered, though" Moaned Slim.

"You'll not feel a thing soon enough" Billy walked over to Slim, took his arm and began leading him up onto the road. "A gallon of beer and a bird; you'll be right."

The others laughed.

"Maybe not the bird." Laughed James, the others joined in. Slim stared at Nutty.

"What the fuck are you laughing at?" Slim shouted. "You're hardly frigging Casanova yourself!"

The others laughed as Nutty looked crest fallen.

"Never mind" said Billy laughing, slapping them both on the back, "There'll be enough for everyone. It's what holidays are about."

"Let's go get 'em!" Cried Michael, leading the way up onto the road.

They all climbed the dune and stepped onto the hot tarmac, turning towards the flashing lights and buzz of the town before them. The air was thick and humid, with a definite whiff of fried food and the saline from the sea as they laughed and joked into Bridlington, their anticipation high. Slim paused at the corner of the road.

"Did anyone turn that stove off?"

Back at the club, the bingo was just finishing and Maureen hadn't made one mark on her bingo card, with Barbara desperately trying to keep up with both of them. Maureen continued to stare in to space, ashen, occasionally mouthing silent words in shock. She pulled out another cigarette and lit it with shaking hands.

"What is it? You look like you've seen a ghost" Barbara pressed her friend, now that the chatter of the club had raised to its previous level. Maureen looked her in the eye.

"The turn: Mickey." She said, taking a long drag of her cigarette.

"What about him?" Asked Barbara

"Don't you remember? 1958?"

Barbara started making the same face her husband had made earlier but the light came on quicker. It dawned. "Oh, bloody hell. Him!"

Maureen blew out a plume of smoke. Hard.

She looked her friend hard in the face and aggressively stubbed the cigarette out in the already overflowing ash tray.

"Oh." Barbara repeated. The lights on the stage had changed and the resident duo had taken up position behind a piano and drum kit respectively. The Chairman was standing again, ready to announce the turn.

"But it was just a little argument that night." Barbara paused. "Wasn't it?"

"Mickey took me home." Maureen spoke quickly.

"You never told me that." Barbara stared at her.

"Why do you think?" Maureen hissed back at her.

Barbara began looking around for Roger, wondering if he knew that Mickey was here.

"Roger doesn't know?" Barbara was amazed at this revelation.

Maureen looked at her friend, reached for another cigarette, saying nothing.

"What happened?"

"I can't remember. I got so pissed after Roger ballsed-up that night, I don't remember nothing."

"But you still got married afterwards so nothing bad could have happened, could it?"

Maureen just continued staring at her friend.

"You wouldn't have done anything bad, 'Reen. I know you. You just wouldn't have done that."

"That's the point, I can't remember!"

The lights in the concert room dimmed as the Chairman announced that night's singer.

"And now, Ladies and Gentlemen, direct from Blackpool all the way to us, here in the Victoria Sailor's……. Mickey McDonald!" Cheers and applause went up as the duo struck up a Neil Diamond number and there, out on the stage, strode a tall, slim man, shiny suit and tie, microphone casually carried in his hand, he smiled at the crowd and waved.

Barbara looked between her friend and the stage.

"Oh fuck." Maureen whispered, not looking at her friend, just staring at the stage. "It's him!"

In the back bar, Roger and Sid both lifted their heads at the sound of Mickey's name being mentioned.

"It's all coming back to me now." Said Sid, recognition slowly dawning on him. "Didn't he kick your arse?"

"Yes, thank you, mate" replied Roger, crossly.

"Well, he buggered off, so you must've done some damage. He never came back to work at the factory either." Said Sid, passing Roger a cigarette.

They both lit up and exhaled gratefully.

"Yet here he is. Like a bad smell."

"I wouldn't worry mate, it's you Maureen married. Not that smarmy tosser."

"I know but…"

"But what? There's nowt to worry about."

Roger looked at him but only announced, "I'm going for a piss." And left the bar. Leaving Sid standing there looking confused.

Roger strode towards the gents toilets in an effort to get away when he was stopped by Dennis in the corridor.

"Now then Roger!" He shouted. "Digs alright?"

"Aye, yes Dennis, they're lovely, thanks" Roger tried to get past him but Dennis blocked his way.

"I see Mickey's on stage tonight. Bringing back memories is it?" He smirked at Roger. Roger slowly turned and took hold of the collar of Dennis' polyester suit. Struggling to get a grip on the cheap, shiny material, Roger moved very close to Dennis' face.

"The last memory you have, Dennis, will be of my fist in your face. Bugger off!" He roughly let go of the suit material and stormed into the gents.

Dennis watched him go, smoothed out his creased collar and sniffed. As the toilet door shut behind Roger, Dennis called after him.

"What you having a go at me for?" He looked about and saw he was alone in the corridor.

Maureen couldn't take her eyes of the stage, watching someone she last saw over twenty years ago, in very different circumstances, bringing back so many memories. She couldn't believe how good he still looked. Barbara was staring at him too, singing along as he belted out hits from the 50's, songs from their formative years.

"He's dishy, isn't he?" Said Barbara onto Maureen's ear only to receive a withering look in response.

Mickey had the audience in the palm of his hand, crooning along and stepping off stage occasionally to take hold of various ladies' hands as he sang directly to them, causing blushes and giggles.

At one point, Maureen thought she had caught his eye but he turned away to finish a song with a flourish, the musical duo taking liberties with the last few bars of the song.

Applause and cheers sounded as he introduced his next number and the duo struck up again. The introduction to 'Pink Sports coat' played up but no voice followed.
A long pause.
The opening bars sounded again. No voice.
Maureen looked up and saw Mickey staring right at her.
"Maureen?"
All eyes in the concert room swivelled and turned to look at the singer and the object of his interest. A few from the chocolate factory were recognising what was going on, those that had been witness to the first incarnation of the scene, back in the late fifties.
Maureen's eyes darted all over and she quickly flicked her hand at Mickey, as if to say, 'not now'.
Mickey put his lips close to the microphone and breathed into it.
"This is for Maureen". The music started and he was off, singing to her.

In the gents, Roger heard this and almost pissed on his own shoes.
"Bastard." He muttered through clenched teeth.

The lads had made it into the Old Town and were trying to decide where to start. It was nearly 9 o'clock now and the pubs were lively, with music pouring into the streets and people standing out in the late evening sun, clasping pints of beer, the condensation dripping down their hands, the sight of which, made them even thirstier.

"We're we off?" Asked Slim, adjusting his waistband, uncomfortable in the heat.

"We'll know when we see it, son." Answered Billy.

"Aye, birds and music; that's what we're after" Laughed Michael.

"Mum and Dad'll be in the club" Said James

"Club?" Billy laughed, "We're not off there. Full of old tarts and grumpy bastards."

"Well, can we just go somewhere? I'm dying of thirst here." Slim moaned.

Billy stepped forward and put his arm around Slim's shoulders.

"Well, let's go and find somewhere befitting your best attire, my son." The others laughed. "Let's not waste your best efforts."

"Piss off."

"Beer, that's what we want." Announced James.

"And that too." Replied Billy.

They walked down South Parade, towards the main front, where they could see dodgems spinning and smell the fried food. They rounded the top of the harbour and looked at the crowds before them. Billy put his arms around Slim and Nutty.

"My friends." He shook them tightly, "Your holiday starts here!"

Before them, the sights were amazing. Spinning rides, vast crowds of people, all drinking and eating, the buzz and throb of disco music reverberated through the soles of their shoes. It felt like the ground was pounding, as women screamed on the rides and men shouted to each other, laughing and joking, The sun was still intense in its heat, the light fold of sea-waves as they hit the sand could be heard in the background and the smell of salt water permeated everything, The concrete of the front was shimmering hot and they felt it through their feet. This was it. Their holiday had begun.

Billy stepped in front of his friends, reached out his arms and smiled.

"Shall we?"

Chapter Fourteen
Memory Lane

"Hello Maureen." The voice was familiar, dripping with sexuality, deep and warm.

Maureen turned and looked into the face of someone she hadn't seen in twenty years,

"Oh my God" Was all she could say.

"You look great" Mickey stood, looking down at her, his six-foot plus frame, encased in stage clothes was a presence that couldn't be ignored.

People milled around them as Maureen queued at the bar, some touched Mickey on the shoulder, congratulating him on his performance.

"Thanks." Maureen said. She didn't know what to do with herself. "Um, you look good too." As she looked up into his eyes.

Oh my God.

She didn't say that, just thought it. The man before her hadn't lost anything of his looks over the last two decades, a bit of grey at the temples and some creases in the brow but still the man she remembered from all those years ago.

"Really." She meant it.

Mickey laughed and smiled, took her hand and kissed it.

"I've never stopped thinking about you." He whispered, leaning forward so close, she could feel his breath on her face.

"Mickey, please don't." she snatched her hand away.

"I'm just telling the truth, darling" He left her hand dangling at the same moment Roger came around the corner.

"Roger!" He called. "Long time, eh?" Mickey stepped away from Maureen, a clear delineation between them.

"Not long enough, lad." Roger grasped Maureen's elbow. "We're going." He stated.

Maureen wrenched her arm from his grasp.

"No, we're not! It's only ten o'clock." She looked between the two men who were squaring up to each other. "It was over twenty years ago! Leave it!" She grabbed her drinks from the bar and left the two of them standing there.

Mickey looked at Roger and held out his hand.

"Look, it was a long time ago, let's leave it now, eh?" His hand dangled in the air.

"I'll leave nowt." Roger hissed in his face. He spun on his heel and began to follow Maureen. Mickey didn't move.

"You learnt how to treat women then, have you?" Mickey called to Roger's back, as he walked off.

Roger froze and turned.

"What?" He asked.

"Somethings don't change, do they?"

"What's your point?"

"Just saying…"

As Maureen put the drinks on table, all she could hear was the sound of glass breaking. She closed her eyes and tensed.

"Mickey and Roger catching up then?" Asked Barbara.

"Not for the first time." Maureen replied.

Chapter fifteen
A Night to Remember

The sound of disco beats were pumping out into the street and the lads moved instinctively towards it. The evening heat was palpable, reflecting off the pavements surrounding the old town. There were patches of sand where people had come straight from the beach, shaken off, and headed towards the bars.

It was nearly nine o'clock and the last vestiges of family life were now leaving, tired kids being dragged away from the amusements, hot parents, pink from the sun, annoyed at having to leave to put the kids to bed, were shouting at them to hurry up.

Slim walked to the first bar and peered inside.

"This one looks alright." He said. Billy followed him in, took a second-long scan of the inside and dismissed it.

"Nah," he said, "not enough women." He walked on, the others following him, with Slim trotting behind to catch up. They got as far as the Half Moon and they halted outside.

"This is the one." Announced Billy.

"Why this one?" James asked, wiping his brow from the heat.

"Birds." He stated.

"How do you know?" Asked Michael.

"I just know." Billy replied.

They stepped inside to an artificial gloom, their eyes taking some time to get accustomed to the change in light. The music was quite loud, mixed with a chatter and buzz from the crowd inside. The back of the pub opened out into a court yard and, beyond the bar, they could see several women catching the last sunshine of the day, sitting on rough benches, made from scaffolding planks and beer crates.

Michael placed his hand on Billy's shoulder.

"You're a fucking genius, mate." He said before walking towards the outside. The others followed, with Nutty turning to Slim and muttering.

"How does he do it?"

"God knows." Slim replied with respect. "But he does it." They moved outside and immediately, Billy was talking to the women, interjected with comments from Michael and James. It was almost instant. Slim and Nutty skirted the fringes of the conversation, smiling in the right places but finding no opportunity to get a word in.

The courtyard was small, but was radiating heat from the day, a few flowers in a tub added to it but, it was just a space to get air, out of the choking smoke in the pub. That being said, the women were busy filling it, puffing away on cigarettes and over-filling the ashtrays.

James turned to Slim.

"Drinks?" He nodded at the bar and returned to the conversation, laughing loudly.

Slim's shoulders dropped but he slunk to the bar anyway. The bar area was busy and people were jostling for position to get the barmaid's attention, waving notes in the air. He stood behind a woman, in order to be better seen, but there was little in it, at his height. The barmaid was flying around, filling glasses and taking money at the same time. It wouldn't be long before he got served. She looked in his direction.

"Yes, love?" She asked, shouting above the noise of the music.

Slim opened his mouth to speak but instead, heard the woman standing in front of him.

"Two halves of cider and a lager and lime please, love." Her voice was high but soft, the barmaid struggling to hear.

"Y'what?" She shouted; she was still fulfilling the last order as she took this one.

"She said, two halves of cider and a lager and lime." Slim spoke over the woman's head, trying to move things along a bit. The barmaid nodded and started pouring. The woman in front of Slim spun around and looked at him.

"Thank you" She smiled and Slim stopped breathing. Looking at him was a beautiful, petite blonde, her hair long over her shoulders, bared by the silk vest she was wearing over her jeans.

"Er, it's a pleasure." He stuttered and blushed, the young woman still looking at him. He shifted from foot to foot until he became aware of the barmaids gaze on him.

"Yes?" She shouted.

"Er," he was struggling to tear his eyes away from the woman before him. "Five lagers please, love"

As the barmaid turned to pick up glasses for his order, his eyes fell on the blonde again.

"On holiday?" he asked, still blushing.

"Sort of." She replied, the three glasses in her hand dripping over her fingers. "I'd best get these to the girls." She said, still smiling but moving slowly off through the crowds.

"Er, OK. Nice to meet you." Slim watched her walk out into the courtyard, where the others were and muttered a small 'thank you God' under his breath.

"That'll be £3.40 love please." The barmaid was standing before him, one hand out and one on a beer pump, filling a glass.

"How much? I only asked for five pints."

"You've got the lasses drinks as well, pet." She still had her hand out.

Slim delved into his pocket and pulled out a fiver, handing it to the barmaid.

"Ta" She spun, rang the till open and got his change. The pound note she handed him were damp and limp as he shoved them back in his pocket. He grabbed a battered tin tray from the edge of the bar and began rounding up the pints onto it. Turning, he saw the crowd he would have to negotiate but, after having been as short as he was since the age of twelve, he knew how to negotiate such things. Head down, voice loud, he got through with people moving politely out of the way of the barrel-shaped person coming at them, full tilt, and not wanting a tray of bitter on their best shirts.

He stepped outside into the sunshine and took a lungful of clear air. Hands reached out to him, taking the pints from the tray and it took a bit of negotiation to not lose his own pint as he became unbalanced.

"You're welcome." He said sarcastically.

"Thanks, Slim!" James called. He was now sitting between two women who were laughing with him. Billy was already in full snog with another and Michael had his hand on a girl's shoulder, smiling and chatting. Nutty was standing alone, like a lost soul and smiled at Slim as he took his pint.

"Alright fella?" He asked, grateful of some company.

"Yeah, yeah." Slim took a long pull on his beer and looked at the woman whose drinks he had just bought. She was chatting away to her two friends but, occasionally, she shot a glance over in Slim's direction. He smiled.

"Who are you smiling at?" Asked Nutty.

"No-one" He replied, unable to tear is eyes away from her. Nutty followed his gaze.

"Have you pulled?" He asked incredulously.

"Eh?" He wasn't paying attention.

"Your fly's undone and your dick is out." Nutty stated.

"Umm?"

"This is serious." He looked over to the girls that Slim was staring at and thought that they weren't half bad. Maybe slightly out of their league but not outrageously so.

"Shall we go over?" He asked, at which Slim suddenly regained hearing.

"What? Are you kidding?"

"No. I'm not. Let's go and talk to women." Nutty ran his fingers through his tight ginger hair, hoped it looked half decent and started moving over to the group.

Slim was frozen to the spot, his eyes like a rabbits in the headlights.

"Come on!" He said. "I'm not going on my own."

"Wait!" Slim was visibly shaking. "What will we say?"

"Let's tell them about making chocolate biscuits at the factory."

"Oh, OK. I can do that." Slim licked his upper lip and moved towards Nutty who immediately put his hand out onto Slim's chest.

"Hang on, hang on. I wasn't serious!"

"Yes, yes, you're right." Slim stopped dead and wiped the sweat from his top lift. "What then?"

"Well how about a general conversation?" He looked down at the sweating Slim before him. He felt sorry for his mate all of a sudden. Maybe this holiday was his chance?

"I'll start it." He sighed, out his hand on his friends shoulder and pushed him gently over towards the girls in the corner.

The girl Slim had been speaking to at the bar saw them coming over, smiled and said something to the others she was with. They giggled with laughter, all looking towards Slim and Nutty, as they tentatively moved forward.

"Oh shit" Whispered Slim through gritted teeth. He had a smile fixed to his face like rigor mortis. Nutty cleared his throat and thrust his shoulders back.

"Come on lad, Dunkirk spirit." He continued moving forward, Slim shuffling along behind him, muttering under his breath.

"Oh Christ, oh God, oh bloody hell." He whispered.

"Shhh" hissed Nutty. "Hello girls!" He said brightly. "Do you mind if me and my friend sit down with you?"

The girls giggled and smiled but shuffled along the seating to make room for the two lads. Nutty looked quickly over the girls. They weren't the best-looking bunch he'd seen but probably within his expectations. It was only the first night anyway, best not to aim too high.

"I'm Nutty." He said.

"I bet you are." One of the girls responded, the rest of them laughing. He smiled.

"It's a nick-name. Me real name is Paul."

"And you prefer Nutty?" She asked incredulously.

"I've known nowt else since school. Even me mam calls me Nutty." He was warming to this girl now. He liked the teasing banter between them. Suddenly he remembered Slim on the periphery.

"Oh, this is me mate, Slim." He pointed over to where he had been standing but he'd gone. Nowhere to be seen.

"Slim?" He called. He stood up and looked around. Nothing. He'd bottled it and run away. Nutty shrugged his shoulders and sat back down. "What's your name then?" He turned back to the girl and carried on chatting. It may just be his night.

In the corner of the bar, Slim sat sipping his pint, trying to get his heart rate back to normal. He'd seen each of the others, tucked away with girls in various areas, at different stages of physical connection. He sighed and leant back onto his chair, closed his eyes, realising how tired he was from the bike ride out here. He wanted to go to bed and the beer wasn't going down too well.

"Can I join you?" A female voice made him open his eyes suddenly and there, in front of him, was the girl from the bar earlier. He sat bolt upright. Her hair framed her face and the light silhouetted her as she leant over to him.

"Ah, er, yes." He stuttered slightly, shuffled along the seat and made room for her.

"I'm Collette." She smiled and held out her hand to him. He looked at it for a second then realised he should shake it. He touched her hand gently, not sure how much pressure to press with, but her shake was firm, which he returned. He didn't want her to think he was soft.

"Slim." He replied, smiling at her.

"I'm sorry?" She asked.

"They call me Slim," He said, realising why she was confused. He looked down at himself and then back at her. "For obvious reasons." He laughed. She didn't; just smiled.

"That's not nice," she replied, "and they're your friends?"

"Aye." He laughed again. "It's just a joke though." He paused, swirling the beer around in his glass. He was at a loss of what to say next.

"Where are you from? I've not seen you around before?"
She asked him gently.

"Oh, from York."

"Ah," she smiled knowingly, "factory fortnight."

"That's it." He paused and smiled at her again but faltered in holding her gaze and went back to his pint.

"Where are you staying?"

"We're camping out of town, on the beach." He looked at her again and saw a slight frown on her face. "It was cheaper than digs." He explained. Paused, realised he sounded cheap at that statement and spoke again. "And it's a bit of an adventure too." He added, hoping she didn't think he was tight.

"Boys will be boys." She nodded. Slim couldn't believe she was still talking to him. There was a lull in the conversation.

"Would you like a drink?" He asked.

"Ah, no thanks." She said and saw the look of disappointment cross his face. She smiled at the reaction, pleased.

"Oh, OK." He spoke, crestfallen. She reached out and touched his arm and a bolt of electricity went through him. He jumped. She felt that too.

"No, it's not that I don't want to," she explained, "It's just that I have to help me mam with the guest house when it's busy." A look of realisation came over him and it dawned on him that he wasn't getting the elbow. She still had her hand on his arm. "I promised I'd be home before eleven, so she's set up for breakfast."

Slim smiled at her and locked eyes.

"Can I walk with you then?" He asked. He gestured around the bar of the pub, at his friends comfortable with girls and ensconced for the evening. "I think I'll go back to the campsite and get an early night."

"OK." She smiled, stood up and put her glass on the table. He followed her lead.

They walked out of the pub, Slim holding open the door for her, remembering all his father had said about being a gentleman. The old sod may have been right after all. For the first time in his life, he was leaving a pub with a woman that wasn't his mother. The magnitude of the occasion wasn't lost on him.

Nor was it lost on Billy who, lifting his head from the neck of the girl he was with, watched Slim leave with a girl. He smiled to himself, storing the image for later. Then he returned to the task in hand.

The club quartet walked back to their lodgings in aggrieved silence, the men at the front and the women at the rear. Sid kept looking over to Roger, trying not to focus on the swelling erupting on his left eye but eager to ask what had happened. Even though he'd been in the bar, it had all happened so fast that he'd only heard the crash of glass, turned, and saw Roger and the turn, being held apart by two burley fishermen.

The speed at which they were walking was fast, Roger eager to get back to the digs, setting the pace.

"You alright Rog'?" Asked Sid tentatively.

"Oh, fucking champion." He replied, spitting slightly from the fat lip he'd got. His brow was furrowed and his mouth set hard as they turned the corner into the street they were staying in. Realising that Maureen had the key, he drew up short of the front gate and waited, arms folded, refusing to look at her, tapping his toe aggressively against the step into the front. Sid stood at his shoulder, watching the girls walk towards them, their heads close together in confidence, whispering. Barbara caught Sid's eye and raised her eyebrows at him. He returned the look, tilting his head slightly at Roger's back. The unspoken conversation made it clear that it could be a long night for them all.

Maureen rooted into her handbag and brought out the key to the boarding house, its wooden fob catching on her purse, causing it to land on the pavement, spilling loose change everywhere. Quickly, Sid and Barbara got to their knees to pick it up, anything to avoid the confrontation that was bound to happen.

"Well?" Roger demanded.

"Well what?" Asked Maureen.

"Are you going to get this bloody door open and let me in?" He continued to tap his toe against the paving slabs.

Maureen paused and looked at him for the first time since the club. His hair was a mess and his eye was swelling. She felt something between anger and pity.

Putting the key in the door, she looked back at her two friends, who were watching her, coins in hands and then she turned to Roger.

"You can sleep with Sid tonight Roger." She said it as a statement, without anger or passion.

"Eh?" He unfolded his arms and looked askance at her.

"I'm staying with Babs." She said.

Roger was stunned.

Maureen looked over at Sid and Barbara, who promptly dropped a halfpence piece and earnestly began looking for it again.

"Why? What have I done?" his arms were outstretched to her, genuinely surprised. "I was protecting you!"

"You were being a twat." She turned the key and pushed open the door. "Again." She held it open with one arm and looked back at her husband and friends who were staring at her.

"I don't need protecting." She said, sadly.

Barbara ran up the path and went in behind Maureen, leaving Roger and Sid standing in the street.

"I don't believe it." Roger said in astonishment. Sid clasped a reassuring hand over his friend's shoulder.

"Come on mate." He said, leading Roger inside.

Inside the house, the girls went to Maureen's room, the door swinging shut with a firm 'click' behind them. Maureen sat at the dressing table and began busying herself with taking off her make-up whilst Barbara sat on the bed and began picking at the candlewick bedspread, trying to think of what to say. She daren't lift her eyes in case she caught Maureen's gaze in the three-sided mirror, so she sighed and carried on picking at the bedspread.

"Go on." Said Maureen, looking at her in the mirror. "I know you want to say something, so let's have it."

Barbara lifted her gaze and caught Maureen's face looking back at her, tears streaming down her face, in triplicate.

"I don't know what to say, love. It's not the night we had planned, was it?" Barbara stood and leaned over, putting her arms around her friend.

Maureen pulled back, sniffed and wiped her eyes with the back of her hand, streaking her mascara in stripes around the sides of her head. Barbara pulled a tissue from a box on the dresser and handed it to her, Maureen blowing her nose into it.

"It'll be alright in the morning." She was trying to convince herself as much as her friend.

"Will it?" Maureen asked between sobs.

"We can sort anything out." Barbara was trying hard to be convincing but it wasn't coming over. She paused, looked around the room and said: "Wait here."

Barbara left the room and Maureen heard from the corridor, footsteps, doors opening, closing and the sound of muffled, questioning voices. Suddenly, the bedroom door opened and Barbara stepped back in, holding two bottles; one gin, one tonic.

She put them on the dressing table with a satisfied thud, walked over to the bedside table and picked up two water glasses before turning back to Maureen and smiling.

"Right lady, you're gonna tell me what the fuck all that was about in the club, then we can start to sort it." Her voice was hard but had a spirited tone to it. Maureen smiled back at her.

"Thank you." She said quietly.

"I want to know what exactly happened in '58 and why Roger has a bee in his bonnet about Mickey." She poured two hefty gins'. "But first," Barbara reached behind her friend for some cold cream and cotton wool. "You're going to get that mascara off your face. It's like sitting here with a frigging cat-burglar in the room."

Maureen looked into the mirror and laughed while Barbara added a splash of tonic into the glasses.

It was going to be a long night.

Chapter Sixteen
A Step Back in Time
York 1958

Roger walked into the works canteen, looking for his
fiancée, Maureen. His hair was heavily greased, trying to
create the quiff that he longed for, but his hair was only just
growing back to how it had been after two years of national
service.

He could see several of his mates on a long table, eating
their lunches and Sid, who was in the middle, waved over
to him to join them, but he wanted to find Maureen.

He could hear music coming from the ladies eating area, the
tinny sound of a transistor sharply coming through the
heavy oak and glass door. Even though he knew he
shouldn't, he pushed it open and saw Maureen amongst her
friends, craning over the radio, the crackling sound of radio
Luxemburg coming through with rock and roll. All of the
young women looked up at him in shock and looked
relieved when they saw it wasn't an overseer staring at
them.

Tracy Hornby, one of Maureen's friends, shouted over to
him.

"Bloody hell Roger, you scared the crap out of us!"

"Sorry" He was suddenly sheepish when confronted by
twenty girls of his own age, all from the chocolate enrobing
room, all looking at him. "I just wanted a word with
Maureen."

Maureen stood and smiled at him. The rest of the girls
began making cooing noises at the sight of the two love-
birds walking out of the room together. As the door shut
behind them, they both heard the radio go back on and a

loud peal of laughter. Roger blushed, knowing it was aimed at something to do with him.

As they turned and looked at each other, Roger gave Maureen a little peck on the cheek.

"Roger!" She exclaimed.

"Sorry. I just wanted to see you." He looked her up and down.

She smiled at him. "Are we still on for tonight?"

"We are darling, yes. Pick you up at 7pm?" He smiled as she nodded at him. He could hear the cat-calls and wolf-whistles from the table his friends were sitting on but he really didn't care. They were just jealous.

Maureen went to open the door but paused as her hand touched the handle. She watched Roger walk over to his friends and thought how caring he was in his possessive way. It was sweet, she thought, and frustrating.

Maureen suddenly decided that she fancied some fresh air before having to go back into the factory, so she turned and headed for the stairs to get outside.

As she reached the doors, she heard a deep singing voice coming from the long, sloping corridor that connected the canteen with the factory, running underground, beneath a main road. She stopped and looked to where it was coming from and saw a tall young man, broad –shouldered, walking purposefully up the slope, towards the canteen. He was wearing blue overalls, not like the other factory workers and carried a tool bag rolled up, which he swung as he walked. As he saw Maureen at the top, he smiled, but didn't stop singing. When he drew level with her, he finally stopped and revealed a white, even smile.

"Hallo pet." His soft Geordie burr echoed down the corridor. "Am I in the right area for some bait?"

"Bait?" Asked Maureen.

"Aye, you know, grub. I'm after me dinner." He was still smiling at her.

"Oh, yes, yes," she replied, flustered. "The canteen's just through there."

"This place is a maze, isn't it? I don't know where I am today."

"Are you new here then?" As soon as she said it, she blushed, realising what a stupid question it was. She fiddled with the curls of hair that peaked out from beneath her cap and wished she could leave but, at the same time, didn't want to.

"Aye pet." He laughed. "Just here for a bit, helping with some work. Then back up the road."

Maureen just smiled back at him, dazzled, then she heard the footsteps of her friends, raucous in their arrival. When they saw Maureen talking to the handsome young man, a hush descended on them.

"I'd better be off." Maureen said, blushing again. Tracey walked over and slid her arm through Maureen's.

"Time to go. The factory is this way." She gently pulled her away from the outer doors and looked the new bloke up and down. "And you are......?" She left the question hanging.

"Michael." He smiled at her and she melted slightly. "But my friends call me Mickey."

"Mickey is it? Well, hello to you. No doubt we'll see you around." Tracey tightened the grip she had on Maureen's arm and pulled. "Come on, you. No need to get us pay docked." She started walking away, Maureen stumbling slightly at the force of Tracey's movement. Mickey watched them go.

"Bye for now!" He called after Maureen. She managed to turn and smile at him before they disappeared out of the corridor and into the factory on the other side.

Mickey turned to walk to the canteen and thought to himself that the day was definitely looking up. He pushed open the doors and stepped into the eating area, ranks of tables were lined up before the hot plate at the back wall. A few of those already eating looked up and appraised the new man whilst the rest were oblivious, busy with their lunch.

Sid leaned forward to Roger and asked, "Who's that?" Roger turned and looked at the new arrival, who was surveying the room and turned back to his plate.

"Dunno, never seen him before. He must be maintenance in that outfit." He carried on eating.

Bridlington 1978

Back in their room, Barbara drained her glass, put it heavily on the dressing table and looked over at Maureen who had finished talking and was looking forlornly into her own glass.

"And that's how you met him?"

Maureen just nodded and carried on staring into her glass.

"Was it love? Sweaty palms and all that?" Finally, Maureen looked at her, began to open her mouth to say something but shut it again before anything came out. She mulled over some words in her head before finally saying. "No, not love. It wasn't that."

"What was it then? Lust?" A sharp look came back at her.

"It wasn't that either. It was…" She paused, trying to think of the right word. "It was connection. That's it. Connection. We connected." She looked proud of herself.

"Connected? I don't understand." Barbara reached for the gin bottle and refilled her glass before leaning over and refilling Maureen's. Maureen sighed.

"Well, you know how, when you meet someone for the first time and you just click? Well, it was like that." Maureen looked at her friend who still looked nonplussed at the explanation. "I can't explain it any better."

Barbara just shrugged, leant back on the pillows and lit a cigarette. Letting out a long stream of smoke she sighed.

"Well, no offence but I can kind of see why Roger is pissed off".

In the other room, Roger and Sid were half way through a bottle of Jonnie Walker whiskey. Roger was gently pressing a wet flannel to his cheek and sucking air sharply through teeth every time it touched.

The room was a facsimile of Roger and Maureen's down the corridor, the same chintz and doilies cluttered the room, the dark mahogany furniture polished to a high shine, making the lamp light overly bright and garish.

"Bastard" he muttered. Roger pushed his cheek towards the mirror and noticed the swelling coming up under his eye. It would be a shiner in the morning.

"Too late for that mate, better let it come out and be done with it. Call it a battle scar". Sid smiled and swirled the whiskey around his glass. He was laid, propped up on pillows, on the bed nearest the sink, watching his friend examining his face.

"Piss off." replied Roger, "Battle scar? More like a fairy slap. This was where I landed. I lost my balance."

"Balance, yes. Hmm."

"Piss off." Repeated Roger and carried on patting his face

"I don't understand why you're carrying this on, anyway. It was over twenty years ago." Sid sipped at the whiskey, wincing slightly at the burn on his throat.

"Look, that wanker was all over Maureen. I'm not having it." Roger put the flannel back in the sink and pulled the plug, the water swirling down the drain with a sucking noise.

"They were just saying hello from what I could see." Sid began picking at the candlewick bedspread, obviously bored.

Roger leaned on the sink edge, his other hand on his hip as he turned to Sid and, uncomfortably, began to tell him the truth.

"Sid, he made out I wasn't good enough for Maureen, never was. And then it all came back to me."

"What did?" Sid raised his head, suddenly interested.

"I've never told no-one this, mate." He looked at the floor, "Not even Maureen." He spoke sadly.

"Told what?" Sid was rapt now, sitting upright, his attention solely focussed on his friend.

"That night, after the fight outside the club, back in the fifties, you remember?" He stared Sid straight in the eye.

"Yes." Sid was getting impatient now.

"Mickey took Maureen home that night. Stayed over. I found the evidence."

"What evidence?" Implored Sid.

"That bastard's flower from his jacket. The one he'd been wearing on stage. It was on Maureen's bedroom floor."

Sid spluttered whiskey into his glass and looked askance at his friend who had turned his face to the floor, embarrassed at admitting this.

"What? Christ almighty, no wonder you hit him. I'd have killed the bastard." Sid swung his legs off the bed and stood to face his friend. Grabbing him by the shoulders, he leaned in. "If I see him, I'll kill him for you."

Roger smiled sadly at his friend and patted his arm in thanks.

"Are you sure, Rog.? I mean are you really sure?"

"Yeah, I'm sure." He turned back to the mirror and continued dabbing his eye. "And nine months later, Michael makes an appearance." Sid did the maths in his head before raising his eyebrows in disbelief.

"No mate, no. You got Maureen pregnant, you were married within two months of that fight; I remember." He paused, thinking of the dates, the celebrations. "Honestly mate, I don't believe it of Maureen."

"Thing is Sid." Roger paused, tears welling in his eyes. "I don't know what to believe"

Chapter Seventeen
Never Let it End

The lights of the amusements, pubs and street lamps all reflected on the tips of the surf as it gently lapped the shore. Some people were walking close to the water's edge but most were strolling along the front, hand in hand or in groups, talking. There was the occasional shout and peal of laughter from the more drunk walkers but mostly, it was evening air and people escaping from the choking fumes of cigarette smoke in the pubs.

Slim was walking next to Collete, his arms behind his back, not knowing what else to do with them, as they walked slowly towards her house. A few times he started to begin a sentence but then stopped, afraid of embarrassing himself but very aware that the longer it was silent, the more awkward it was becoming.

Eventually, she stopped, placing her hands on the Victorian railings that topped the sea wall and looked out towards the gentle rolling waves, the crest of which were only just visible from the harbour lights.

"Slim?" Collette breathed the words, the sudden cold of the night air highlighting them in mist.

"Yeah? Are you OK?" Startled, Slim reached out to the railings and stood next to Collette, wondering what was coming. Expecting the brush-off and thinking to say goodbye first and head back to the camp-site.

Suddenly, he felt her hands on his as she reached over. Taking his hands in hers, she pulled him away from the barriers and moved in front of him. Looking him in the eye, she pulled him closer to her. He stopped breathing.

"Slim?"

"Yes, Collette?"

"Shall we get some chips?"

Slim's smile went wide and, looking in her eyes, he felt
something that he hadn't before. His heart was fast and,
despite the breeze, he felt hot and the sweat trickled down
his back. His hands were tacky as he held hers, wondering
if he should be touching her, scared to be doing so. She
smiled, and turned toward the promenade, where the smell
of frying was billowing along with the evening breeze. She
led him by the hand and down the wide pavement, Slim
trotting behind her.

The chip shop was tucked into a back street, the only bright
light in an otherwise dark row of terraces. The light
reflected out onto the street, casting several people in pools
of yellow neon, as they moved back and forth, collecting
newspaper-wrapped chips, chattering with each other.
Laughter rippled across the tarmac as Slim was steered into
the shop by Collette, the light pressure on his hand guiding
him in.

The smell of hot lard hit him like a cloud, the sizzle from the
fryers creating a backdrop, punctuated by the server calling
out orders to the fryer, who was half-hidden behind the
gleaming stainless-steel range. Smoke and steam enveloped
him occasionally, like a pantomime villain, appearing from
the clouds of hot steam from the vast fat fryers.

"Chips!" He Shouted. The clouds of steam moving with his
voice.

"Right!" The server shouted back. She never took her eyes
off the tower of paper in front of her, a stack of greaseproof
and one of cut newspapers. Her left-hand thumb was
coloured black from the ink of the sheets of newspaper she

constantly lifted, licking her thumb every time, lifting her scoop, laden with hot chips, onto the newspaper and, with three swift moves, wrapping them tightly, before handing them over to the waiting hands on the other side of the melamine counter.

Ten minutes later, they were outside, their hands filled with paper and hot chips, the smell of vinegar and salt pervaded the air as they shuttled hot potato around their mouths, the chips too hot to eat but too nice to leave alone. They walked down terraced streets, the Victorian buildings high, four and five stories, most of them converted to guest houses and each one showing a 'no vacancies' sign in the window. Eventually, they stopped at a red-painted house, in the middle of the row and Collette stopped, turning to look at Slim. Her lips were shiny from the chips and she screwed up the paper and tossed the ball of print from hand to hand, suddenly uncomfortable.

"This is me!" She announced brightly. The house behind her was brightly lit, enough to guide itinerant residents home from the town. It was a stunning house, reaching high into the night sky, with random lights on in the windows. Slim suddenly found himself in no-man's land, wondering what to do next.

"Erm, I've had a great night. Thanks." He carried on eating. They shuffled their feet on the pavement.

"Well, I er…." Collette looked up at the door.

"Oh yes, yes. Well, good night. It's been a pleasure." He held out a hand, greasy with chip lard. Collette reached out and held it. Suddenly, the front door of the house opened and a man stood on the doorstep.

"Collette? What time do you call this?" A man's voice called out, echoing down the street. Slim jumped.

"Well, er, I'll be off then. Maybe see you in the week?" His hand was still being held and suddenly, it was pulled towards Collette. She pulled him in and kissed him full on the lips. The wrapper in his hand dropped to the floor. "Goodnight." She smiled and dropped his hand, before running up the steps and into the house.

The man's voice from behind the door could be heard muttering, with Collette responding in kind.

Slim stood dumbfounded, rooted to the spot. His mouth broke into a smile, then a grin then a beaming, idiotic, opened mouthed amazed face. He was stood in a pool of street light and felt like the star of the show, ready to perform.

"Well, fuck me." He mumbled, carried on smiling, turned and made to walk down the street, disappearing from the light and into the darkness of the street.

The street returned to silence, only the distant noise of the waves could be heard, broken by occasional shouts from drunken holiday makers.

A hand appeared into the pool of streetlight and picked up the wrapper, still containing some chips. Then disappeared. "Well, fuck me…" the words were lost in the darkness.

Not long later, sand could be heard being displaced around the tent the lads were now asleep in, as Slim staggered in the darkness, trying to find the zip to his own bed for the night. He shuffled his feet across the sand, knowing that there would be obstacles in the way, not least, the guy ropes and he couldn't see a thing. Nothing.

His left foot hit beer cans, which scuttled across the sand, connecting with each other, making the most obscene noise. He tried to shush them, but they didn't listen.

"Shut up!" A drowsy voice came out of the tent, it sounded like Michael. Thank God. A guiding light.

"Michael?" Slim whispered hoarsely.

"Fuck off!" His voice got louder.

"I'm lost mate!" He called out, in a whisper barely quieter than a shout. Reaching out, he could feel canvas and suddenly, his fingers found the zip.

"Oh, thank Christ." He whispered. The zip ratcheted up and he stepped inside.

"Who the fuck is that?" Nutty's voice called out, slurred from drink and sleep.

"It's me: Slim." He whispered back. "You OK?" He began stripping his cords and shirt, his feet looking for his sleeping bag by means of wide sweeping.

"Eh? Where've you been?" Nutty sat up and tuned on a torch, shining it straight at Slim.

"Ah, fuck off!" Slim wrapped his arms around his face, shielding his eyes from the sudden light.

"Did you get lucky?!" He cried, "We've all been wondering where you went."

Slim shuffled into his sleeping bag, rocked right and left to get his feet to the bottom.

"A gentleman never tells." He said, smiling. He wrapped his arm over his eyes. "Turn the bastard light out."

Nutty snapped the torch off and laid his head back down, chuckling to himself.

Slim opened his eyes in the dark and stared at nothing. He couldn't stop thinking about her. Sleep wouldn't come easy tonight.

For once, he was glad of it.

Chapter Eighteen
The Morning After

Roger's face was stuck to the pillow. He'd been drooling in the night. He could feel the weight of Sid in the bed next to him, the warmth of his body. For a split second he thought it was Maureen but then it all came back to him, the night before, the fight and he realised where he was.

He groaned as he turned over. His head was cracking with pain.

The empty bottle of Johnnie Walker stood on the bedside table, a reminder to the pain from the night before. And now. In his head.

He shuffled his weight over to the edge and grabbed a glass of water, relieved that he'd had some foresight the night before. It went down in one. His head hit the pillow again and hoped he would sleep some more but, suddenly, Sid's arm came over and wrapped itself around him.

"Sid?"

"Erm?" A drowsy mutter came back.

"Sid!" Roger shouted. Sid grunted, farted and rolled over, away from Roger, face to the wall. "Jesus." He muttered.

Reaching over to the bedside table, he lifted his watch and checked the time. It was nine o'clock. They had to be out by ten.

"Oh fuck!" He jumped out of bed, still in his shirt and trousers and ripped back the covers, revealing a naked Sid. "What the fuck?" He shouted.

Sid jumped up, bleary-eyed, and tried to focus on his friend. "Eh? What's going on?" Sid asked, trying to place himself.

"Why the fuck are you in the buff?" Roger spluttered.

"Er, I got too warm in the night. What time is it?" Sid placed his hands around his privates, suddenly embarrassed, realising where he was. Not with his wife; that's for sure. "Time we were gone, mate. It's past breakfast. Come on." Roger started running water in the sink, winced at the sight of his new black eye and splashed his face. He grabbed his razor and wiped shaving foam onto his chin. Sid stood up and started looking for his trousers. Roger caught sight his bare arse in the mirror and grimaced. "Christ." He muttered.

In the room across the corridor, Maureen was brushing her hair in the dressing table mirror whilst Barbara was retching in the sink.
"Fucking gin." She said between heaves.
Maureen looked at her in the reflection in the mirror and carried on applying mascara.
Barbara wiped her mouth on the towel and Maureen made a mental note to take them all downstairs to be washed.
When they were both dressed and ready, pale-faced and feeling nauseous, they put their ears to the door to hear if the two men were up and about.
Nothing.
"Are you ready?" Asked Maureen.
Barbara just nodded, an apprehensive look on her face.
Maureen gripped the door handle firmly.
"Let's just get straight out of here. We're not stopping for nothing."
She pulled the door open sharply, stuck out her head and quickly scanned left and right.

"Right, we're clear. Let's go." She reached back for Barbara's hand and pulled her out of the door, which clicked into place behind them.

They tip-toed across the landing and down the stairs, hoping that they wouldn't be seen, before opening the porch door to the guest house and out onto the street. They waited until they got to the end of the street and around the corner, then they finally breathed.

"Right," asked Barbara, "what now?"

Chapter Nineteen
British Bulldog

"Slim!" Billy's voice boomed through the tent opening, the fetid stink of sweat mixed with condensation caused him to grimace and snap his head back to get some fresh air before putting his head back in to wake his friend. "Slim! Wake up!"

A movement in the sleeping bag, followed by a groan and then an arm flopped out. There was condensation dripping down the inside of the tent, the outside sun already heating the air inside to unbreathable levels.

There were socks and pants strewn around with several empty beer cans on Nutty's side, which clanked as Slim stretched out his legs in the bag, moving like a slug across the tarpaulin floor, groaning at the effort of the stretch.

"Slim! Come on, you lazy twat! Breakfast!"

Slim stretched an arm, followed by another and, finally, raised his head to look bleary-eyed at Billy.

"Morning." He was still smiling.

"Good night was it, son?" Billy grinned at him.

"I've had worse." Slim grinned back.

"You sly bugger" Billy laughed and let the flap of the tent fall.

Outside on the sand, the rest of the lads were spread out, their kit spread even further, whilst Nutty was leaning over a primus stove, trying to fry eggs, with the sea wind blowing the flame flat, he was cursing and laughing at the same time as the lads ribbed him on his culinary skills; or lack of.

The sun was already heating the sand to an uncomfortable temperature, Nutty hopping from foot to foot, trying not to burn the soles of his feet, the others were laid out on towels, knees to their chests, already in their swimming trunks and waiting to eat.

"I'd like my eggs sunny side up!" Michael shouted from the side lines, he was smoking and had already started on the lager.

"Sunny side my arse" Nutty retorted.

Some cooked bacon was laid out on some newspaper, fat soaking through the sheets, keeping warm in the heat of the morning sun. James was hovering with two slices of bread, bacon draped across, desperate for something to eat.

"Come on fella! I'm starving."

"Alright, Christ, it's not bloody cooking!" Nutty flipped the egg over, held it down with his fork, then flipped it onto James' bread. "There you go, soldier!"

"What the fuck is this?" The uncooked white of the egg was pouring out of his bread, soon followed by the yolk, onto the sand.

"Your breakfast, you ungrateful tosser." Nutty flicked the fork at him, lard flying out on to James' bare chest.

"Arrgh! That bloody hurt." He rubbed the patch of skin where the lard had hit but quickly shoved the egg sandwich in his mouth, regardless.

"It'll bloody hurt even more if I shove this fork up your arse. Bon appetite, wanker." Nutty flipped off the primus stove and walked over to the others. "So, what's the score today then?"

Billy lifted his head from his towel and looked at Nutty. "What do you want to do?" His head flopped back lazily. "Get out of the way, you're blocking the sun!"

"Are we lying here all day, frying?" He asked, stepping sideways.

"It's the only fucking thing fried here." James was still wiping yolk from his chin and hands.

Suddenly, the flap of a tent opened and out stepped Slim, blinking in the brightness. As one, the rest of the lads began jeering and clapping at him. Slim grinned sheepishly, held his palm above his eyes to block the sun and saw his friends, all laid out on towels, reddened by the sun. Only Nutty was wearing a t-shirt but he had his trunks on, his long pale legs, stippled by ginger hairs were gangly, his trunks tight around his backside.

"Now then stranger!" He called over. "Get your trunks on and get yourself out here."

"What's for breakfast?" He asked, walking over to them all.

"Sod breakfast. What happened last night?" Michael was sitting upright on his towel. All the others followed his lead, staring at Slim as he shuffled his feet in the sand, embarrassed.

"I'm hungry." He said quietly, staring down at the sand.

"Worked up an appetite, did you? What was she like?" Michael grabbed a handful of sand and threw it in Slim's direction.

"Sod off. It wasn't like that. I just took her home."

"And then what? A knee-trembler against the front door?" Michael laughed at him, the others followed, all except Billy.

"Shut up, Michael." Billy cut the laughter off and stood up, walking over to Slim. "Ignore them."

"It wasn't like that." Slim muttered as Billy put his arm around his shoulders.

"I know son, I know." He led him away from the others, who were still sniggering.

"A local lass?" Billy asked, walking Slim towards the flat of the beach, where the breeze was fresher.

"Yeah," Slim was squinting into the sun and already feeling hot in his cords from last night, "her mam and dad own a guest house in town."

"Wow, I'd shut the door on that one mate!" He looked at Slim, a wry smile on his unshaven face. Slim smiled back.

"Piss off." He replied, shoving his friend gently.

They walked further out on the beach and could see the crowds of families, laid out beyond the shoreline. Balls were being thrown up in the air and laughter was carried on the wind, the laughter of children, men and women. The sun was bright and hot but a breeze was picking up the loose sand and swirling it around, hitting the striped windbreakers that dotted the beach.

"She works there, then. Running the place?"

"Just helps out. She works at the Sarah Lee factory, making cakes."

Billy cried with laughter and slapped Slim on the back, knocking him forward.

"Bloody hell, mate. A cake maker. Your perfect woman."

Slim condescended to smile at that, then laughed himself.

"You're not wrong on that one, lad." Slim looked across the sand to the others laid on their towels, then again towards the families laughing and having a good time on the beach. "I want to find her again, Bill. I want to take her out and… oh, I don't know what to do."

Billy sighed and placed his hand on his friend's shoulder.

"You do, lad. You do."

"What?"

"If it's meant to be; it's meant to be." Billy stood with his hands on his hips, feet planted in the sand, while he looked all around at the scenes on the beach, keen to see if there were any groups of girls already out in the sun.

"What if she doesn't want to? Oh Christ, Bill. I can't handle this." Billy took hold of his friend's arms and forced him to look into his face.

"Now listen, you are perfectly capable of talking to a lass and letting her..." He paused and left the sentence hanging.

"Letting her what?" Cried Slim, expecting something crude to follow. Billy sighed, took a step back and looked intensely at his friend.

"Letting her get to know you!"

Slim looked down and kicked out at the sand.

"That's what I'm afraid of." He mumbled

Billy folded his arms and stared out to sea. "I think we need something to take your mind off this"

"Like what?" Slim was excavating a hole with his toe, not meeting his friend's eye.

"Something that'll get the old blood pumping!" Billy started jogging on the spot. "Come on, a bit of competition!"

"Eh?" Slim lifted his head and looked at Billy. Billy turned to look back at the others who were laid out on the sand, sweating in the sun. They were beginning to throw sand at each other, bored already.

"There is only one thing I can think of." Billy carried on.

"British Bulldog!" Billy put his hand on Slim's shoulder and smiled.

"Ah fuck off. Really?"

"Really." Billy turned to the others and shouted. "Oi! You lot! Get your arses over here!" he walked over to them, leaving Slim in the hot sand.

"Shit." Slim said under his breath then followed him up the beach.

Chapter Twenty
Drowning Sorrows

Roger took a long pull on the pint of bitter that Sid had put in front of him.

"You'll have to talk to her, you know." Sid lit a Players cigarette, exhaled deeply and threw the pack across the table towards his friend. Roger pulled a cigarette from the pack, lit it and blew smoke back at Sid, who coughed then laughed. "You can't spend the next fortnight not talking to your own wife."

They were sitting in a pub after walking into the old town, having crept from from the guest house, not wanting to see Maureen and Barbara. Neither had the stomach for breakfast and Roger didn't feel like eating, so they'd walked and waited for the pubs to open. Sid looked wretched and Roger's face held a permanent frown, last night's scrap replaying over and over in mind.

Set away from the front, the pub had a couple of hardened locals nursing pints in the shadows but no holiday makers, except Roger and Sid who tucked themselves into the snug, in a bid to avoid conversation from others. There was no music playing, the only sound came from the landlord moving bottles around and cleaning the brasses on the bar.

"I just can't even look at her at the moment, Sid." He was simmering with anger but also close to tears at the thoughts that were rolling around his head. His hair was tousled, roughly combed and his eye was swollen and bruised, adding to the bags that were more pronounced than ever.

"But what is she supposed to have done? I don't understand. You had a push and a shove with someone in bar, carrying something from twenty years ago and you've shut down on Maureen, who wasn't even there, and now you're giving her the cold shoulder."

"It's what he didn't say." He paused. "What's never been said."

"I don't understand."

"No, I doubt you would." Roger spoke softly; sadly.

Sid banged his pint down in exasperation, causing the Landlord to look up as the ashtray rattled. Sid smiled at him and nodded, before turning back to Roger.

"You're not making any sense at all."

Roger leaned forward, over the table, conspiratorially and whispered. "Do you remember when Maureen told me she was pregnant with Michael?"

"Vaguely." Sid leaned forward too, frowning, trying to understand.

"It was the month after I had that punch-up with Mickey McDonald outside the club in York, wasn't it?"

"Mebee, I don't see…"

"And he had taken her home that night, hadn't he." Roger sat back again, shakily putting his cigarette back between his lips. Sid still leaned forward, brow furrowed, his lips working silently, trying to understand what Roger had just said. Slowly, the frown lifted and it dawned on him.

"You mean….?"

"That's exactly what I mean." Roger growled.

Sid fell back into his chair, a look of shock on his face. "I can't believe it, Rog. There's no way Maureen did the dirty on you."

"Adds up though doesn't it? Michael is tall and blonde. Not like me, is he?"

"That doesn't mean anything."

"Doesn't it? It fits." He stubbed out his cigarette and sat back in his chair.

"Only because you're making it fit." Sid drained his pint. "Another one?"

Across town, Maureen took a sip of her coffee and wiped the froth from her top lip. Barbara was just staring at her. They were sat in Notoriani's coffee bar, near the front, trying to revive themselves from last night. The café was all chrome and melamine, the hissing steam of the coffee machine drowning out all conversation.

Barbara looked rough, her skin pale under her make-up, she was nursing a gale-force hangover from the gin the night before and she nursed her coffee gingerly, not sure whether to drink it, or to go the toilet and throw up.

"You ok?" Maureen asked. Barbara was trying hard not to retch, gulping air and swallowing, her coffee was going cold, untouched.

"Feel like shit, to be honest."

"Yeah, I know what you mean." Maureen stirred a sugar into her coffee. She wondered where Roger was, worried about his state of mind. She wondered where her sons were too, somewhere out on the sands, no doubt, having a great time, oblivious to what was happening with their parents. Looking out of the window, she watched multiple people, families, all laughing, joking and having a good time. They were laden with bags and balls, all heading to the beach. Where had the years gone?

"You'll have to talk to him you know." Barbara had managed a couple of sips of coffee. "You can't leave it like this."

"I know; I know." Maureen drained her coffee and took hold of her friend's hands. "Why, after all these years did he have to show up?"

"Pleased to see him though, weren't you?" Barbara looked up from under her fringe and winked at her.

"Bugger off," Smiled Maureen, "it was a shock though. Twenty years, bloody hell. Where did that go?"

Barbara sighed, and nodded.

"I just can't believe Roger doing that. Why now?" Barbara said, stirring her coffee absentmindedly; the froth disintegrating into nothing.

Slim walked slowly across the sand, to the natural gap left by the outgoing tide, away from the holiday makers. It was a mixture of wet sand and running water, heading to the sea. Families were camped behind him, but the channel was clear, perfect for a game of Bulldog.

He could faintly hear the voices of his friends, being enlisted into the game by Billy, he kept on walking, muttering to himself.

"What a bloody stupid idea! Bulldog in this heat! Why in the name of Christ am I doing this?"

His mutterings didn't go unheard.

Families and groups of youths heard him, looked at each other and smiled. Bulldog? On a hot day? They were bored already. Most families had been kicked out of their B&B's by 10am and couldn't return until tea time. Harassed by kids and older parents, everyone was trying to make the most of the sun and count down the hours until the pubs opened.

The whisper passed down the line...Bulldog!

Slim kept walking. He was counting steps. 89, 90, 91....
What he didn't realise were the footsteps of the people
behind him, looking to join in as they trotted from their
towels and headed towards the lads from the factory who
smiled at the sight of the stream of people coming to add to
the offensive line. They looked between each other grinning
and over at where Slim was finishing his counting,
oblivious to what was about to happen.

Slim got to 100 and then moved from left to right, drawing a
line in the sand. He was still muttering to himself, unaware
to everything going on behind him. Suddenly, a shout went
up behind him. He heard Billy calling.

"You ready, fella?" His voice seemed a long way off to Slim,
slowly, he turned around, wondering how far their run-up
was going to be.

What he saw before him; he couldn't believe.

There was still a low sand haze caused by the sea fret as the
water heated in the midday sun. In it, Slim could see the
shimmering outlines of people lined up and milling around,
the sun behind them, causing their shapes to be blurred. He
lifted his palm to shield his eyes.

Suddenly, the ground began to shake and sand raised up as
a crowd began to stampede.

A roar went up, carried on the breeze from the sea.

Slim lowered his hand slowly.

"Oh Fuck..."

"ARRGGHHHHHHH!!" It hit like a hurricane as scores of
bodies raced past Slim, kicking sand in the air, blinding him
temporarily.

It was like a wind tunnel, the vacuum caused by all these
people racing past fixed him to the spot as though he were

anchored. He struggled to breathe as the dust rose around him, coughing out sand and flapping his hands to clear some air. Bodies rushed by him, some close enough to touch him and he realised, if this wasn't going to turn into an almighty piss-take, he was going have to reach out and fell someone. Slim shut his eyes tight and clenched his fists. Not today. Not him.

He reached out and grabbed the next body that came by him, spinning his weight over into the sand, he felt the body of someone fall next to him.

One down.

Slim scuffed his feet in the sand, made a toe-hold and propelled himself up. He still had his eyes closed against the whipped dust that was hitting his face. Again, he reached out his tensed arms and felt the crump of a body against him. Down again.

Two down.

Suddenly, the dust began to settle as everyone passed and made it to the other side. Slim opened one eye, looked around him, then opened the other. They were amassed like the rank of an army on the further side of the beach. Bloody hell, he thought, where were this lot from?

He wiped his eyes and looked at the two he had brought down earlier. A middle-aged man with a pot belly and a teenager. Both looked back at him, wide-eyed and shocked at the onslaught they had been a part of. Sand began to settle around them as the two new-comers suddenly realised that they were on Slim's side now, facing the ranks of holiday makers that had made it to the other side of the line. They pushed back their shoulders and turned to stand alongside Slim, like long-lost comrades facing a mutual enemy.

"Ready?" Slim asked softly, without looking at them.

"Ready." They confirmed.

Slowly, softly, they moved as if by some unspoken order and spread out along the line, at all times, staring hard at the line of figures lined up fifty yards away. They could see their feet pawing the sand, chests heaving in the heat and the exertion, like bulls in the ring, getting ready to run at them.

The atmosphere was tense, each side waiting for the other to move, like a Mexican stand-off.

All around them, families were gathering to watch, excited by all the action, the most they had seen all holiday. They'd had three days and nights of kids screaming and second-rate cabaret in the clubs. Here was real action.

Ranks of people, gathered to the left and right, all aimed at three hapless individuals, who stood in no-man's land, waiting for the onslaught.

Slim looked to his left and saw the families gathered. On the left, the North Sea, lapping lazily onto the sand in the heat. It was like the charge of the Light Brigade, caught on all sides, the only the option was to remain fast and take it all on.

Feeling as he did after last night, he felt like he could take on the world. Bring it on.

The sand began to rumble.

The thump of feet in hot sand began to make its way to Slim and his new two compatriots, who looked at each other, first in fear, then in an affirmation of solidarity, they took on a steely resolve.

"Let's get these fuckers." Slim said to them both as a cloud of hot, powdered sand began rising, channelled between the holiday makers on the left and the sea to the right, it came straight at them.

The youngster screamed first.

"Just reach out and grab!" Shouted Slim.

"Arrghh!!! Get them!!" The middle-aged guy that had joined them shouted as sand and dust rained over them, followed by the thud, thud, thud of bare feet on the sand. It was all a dirty, cloudy melange of bodies, limbs and grunting bodies, rising and falling, crossing the line of British Bulldog.

Slim and his new mates reached out and grabbed, as asked, and bodies fell, left and right. Things were grabbed that maybe shouldn't have been, but it was a life-and-death situation, that was how they felt, as people went down hard into the sand, with screams and cries.

When the cloud of sand cleared, Slim stood and looked around. There were seven more people gathering themselves and standing up, slapping the sand off themselves. All eyes were raised towards Slim.

He stared back. Took one look at the crowd that had gone past them, then looked at his increasing number of soldiers. He narrowed his eyes and gathered them around him.

"This is war." He rubbed his hands.

Chapter Twenty-One
Days that last forever...

Maureen buried her toes deep into the warm sand. She could hear screaming and laughter from somewhere further down the beach, but she ignored it. No laughter here.

Next to her, Barbara was laid out in the sun, her hangover abating, she had pushed down the top of her dress to reveal her shoulders to the sun and pulled up her skirt as far as her knickers. She was frying.

The heat was stifling and the gentle lap of the waves only fuelled Maureen's bad mood. She didn't know what to do for the best and, if she was honest, she felt lost without Roger.

No: wait. Not lost. Like something was missing.

"Where do you think they are?" Maureen asked out loud, not really directing it at her friend.

"What?" Barbara pulled down her sunglasses to look at her friend but the sudden glare of the sun in her eyes made her fall flat, back onto the sand. "Oh fuck." A wave of nausea washed over her, making her swallow hard, over and over, until the wash of saliva subsided. She raised her hand in submission and placed it on her friend's shoulder. Unable to talk, she just groaned.

"I just wondered where they were?" Maureen pivoted on her bum, directing the question at her.

"They'll be in a pub somewhere." Barbara muttered back her. "Like we should be."

Roger placed another pint of bitter in front of Sid as they sat in the lounge bar of another pub, having moved on from the old town, getting steadily drunk and attempting to make sense of things. The bar was practically empty, except for three old guys sitting at the bar, not talking, just reading newspapers. The bar maid was slouched against the back fridges, chewing gum slowly, loudly.

"Where the fuck are they?" Roger slurred slightly whilst Sid sipped the froth off his beer.

"They'll be alright. At the beach, probably." Sid looked around the bar and could see chinks of sunlight through the heavy curtains. He wished he was at the beach, in the sun, the only reason he was here on holiday.

Sid sat his glass back on the table heavily and looked at Roger. He noticed the grey edges to his badly shaven face, a couple of cuts and his heavy, tired eyes. His hands were shaking as he lit another cigarette, another one in a countless number.

"Look Rog, what are you going to do when you do see her? It's all a mess, mate."

"I don't know. I just don't know." He blew out a stream of blue cigarette smoke. "I just want to know she's alright, and.." He paused.

"And?"

"That she's not with him." He grabbed his glass angrily, slopping beer across the table.

"With him? Are you mad?" Sid began trying to mop up the beer with mats, dabbing at the puddle.

"Fucking furious mate!"

"No, I mean, she wouldn't do that to you."

Roger put his glass down again and looked his friend in the eye.

"She has before."

Maureen and Barbara strolled along the front, past the amusement arcades and the fish and chip stalls, Barbara trying hard not to retch at the smell of hot dripping. Her shoulders were red from the sun and her head was banging. Desperate for some shade, she took hold of Maureen's elbow and held her back.

"Please, can we go somewhere and get a drink? I'm dying here."

Maureen looked around, people were milling around, lazy with the heat, kids running in and out of the arcades, seagulls padding around, looking for dropped chips and she realised she felt exhausted, not wanting to be a part of it anymore.

"Yes, let's get in somewhere. I'm knackered."

They walked from the front into the side streets where the shade was cooler. The high, five-storey Victorian houses threw long shadows across the road, leaving a patch of sunlight that shone on the ornamental gardens that ran down the centre of the road. Pensioners were sitting on the benches, eating ice creams, wrapped in coats and hats, not talking to each other.

"Oh, for Christ's sake, let's get out of here. Go home, anything, just away from here." Maureen strode purposefully towards the Old Town, determined to get away.

"Whoa, whoa, whoa," Barbara stopped walking and reached out to her. "You can't run away. You need to talk to him. Sort things out."

"Sort things out? He's gone crazy about this whole Mickey thing!"

"Do you blame him?" Barbara was breathing hard, beads of sweat on her brow.

Maureen looked at her, paused.

"No, I don't but he could start by bastard listening!" She strode forward, determined. The pensioners were watching them, getting the most entertainment they'd had all week. Barbara wiped the sweat from her brow and stood straight to look Maureen in the eye. Grabbing her by the shoulders, she held her gaze firmly.

"Look. You need to talk to him and put this right. Whatever happened twenty years ago, I don't know but, you need to explain it to him." She rested her hands on her knees, breathing hard, exhausted by the exchange.

Sid placed another two pints on the table top, wafting away layers of blue smoke, he could barely see beyond them.

"Right," He said, sitting down decisively, "This is what we are going to do."

Roger had his head laid on his arms, his chin resting on the folds of his arms, staring straight ahead. Not listening.

"We are going to go back to the boarding house, get ourselves a hot bath each, sober up and face those women." He paused. "Our wives."

"And do what?" Roger was slurring now, topped up from the previous night, he was well on the way. Sid realised he was now duty adult and responsible for his friend.

"Mate, come on, drink up. We're off for a kip and a bath. Not in that order."

"Fuck off." Roger was drooling onto his arm now.

"Right-oh mate. Off we go." He reached under Roger's armpits and lifted him up from the table. Balancing him on his shoulder, he put cigarettes and lighters into his pocket and pivoted Roger around the table, trying not to spill the drinks. He failed.

"Sorry love!" He called over to the barmaid. She looked up nonchalantly and waved her hand. She'd had worse.

Out on the street, the sudden flash of sunlight blinded them momentarily. They staggered backwards, onto the polished tiles of the pub, Sid falling under Roger's weight. Righted, he pointed them both in the direction of the boarding house, hoping that they would make it.

"Come on old son. Let's get home." He pointed them in the right direction and staggered into the afternoon sun.

Chapter Twenty-two
When the past come calling...

York July 1958

Roger strolled down Coney Street, walking with a swagger of confidence. He stopped outside the windows of Leak and Thorpe's, the big department store, and checked his reflection. Taking out a comb, he swept his hair back and nodded. His hair was getting back to where it used to be before his two years National Service, long on top and a DA at the back. He put his comb back into his back pocket, flicking off the excess Brylcreem first, smiling at himself, then carrying on walking down the street.
Tonight, was going to be a great night.
He checked the ring in his pocket, tight against his chest as he strolled on to Museum street, past groups of people on a night out. He recognised a few from the factory and from the railway yards, nodding hello and raising his hand. Walking to the Theatre, he saw Sid under the eaves of the building, drawing on his cigarette. A few buses were trundling past and a few hardened tourists were taking photographs, down the street towards York Minster. There was more each year, Roger smiled, watching them trying to find their way in a crooked, medieval city, displaced by their lives in American grid systems. Nothing made sense. Yanks thought Roger. He'd seen enough of them in Germany on manoeuvres.
"Sid!" He shouted across the street, a few faces looking at him, wondering what the noise was about. Sid looked over and smiled, his newly-grown quiff gleamed in the evening

light, heavily greased and perfect, he dared not move his head too much in case it fell to one side.

"Rog! You ready?" Sid shouted back and stepped out from under the eaves of the theatre, jogging across the road, holding his quiff all the while. Both were wearing sports coats with vast shoulder pads, making them look wider than they really were, their thin legs encased in drain-pipe trousers and their winkle-picker shoes, gleaming with polish, the army having given them some skills useful in the world.

"I'm ready mate; are you?" Sid carried in his inside pocket, a ring for Barbara too. They had agreed for it to be a big celebration, both engaged on the same night.

What could go wrong?

They strode past the art gallery and around the corner until they reached Mary Gate, the old gate house stood proud on the corner, looking lost amongst all the other buildings. Turning the corner, they saw a steady stream of people walking towards the club, amongst them, they could make out the backs of both Maureen and Barbara, tottering down the steep hill on heels, arm in arm, heads close together in conversation.

"Shall we go and catch them?" Asked Sid, starting to look to cross the road. A hand on his arm stopped him.

"No, wait. Give them a chance to get in and sat down. Let them wonder where we are."

Sid looked at him confused and then realisation crept onto his face.

"Ah, yes, let them wait. Good thinking." He looked over the road and saw the crowd clear as they walked towards the Post Office Club. "Shall we get some Dutch courage?"

"Aye, let's go and have a couple before we go in. Let them get the bingo over with."

They stepped over the road and into the Minster Inn, a small, dark bar shrouded with curtains. It smelt of stale beer and detergent and, in the various snugs, sat old men, nursing pints and whiskey chasers, not talking.

The only sound was the loud ticking of a brewery clock on the wall. The time on it was wrong. Roger and Sid looked at each other, Sid nodding back towards the door as if to leave when, suddenly, a blue-rinsed perm came through the curtains.

"Yes loves?" The Landlady had poked her head through and was staring at them both through watery, myopic eyes. She had no teeth in and there were remnants of her dinner down her front, which, by the smell, involved cabbage.

"What the f….?" Sid jumped back, grabbing Roger by the sleeve.

"Two pints is it, loves?" She smiled a gummy smile, her toothless mouth surrounded by mis-applied lipstick.

"Er, yes love, please." Roger tried to be polite, feeling trapped, he quickly looked at Sid who was shaking his head slowly, begging him to leave and taking him too.

"Right, Coming up." She shuffled behind the bar, Roger could see her arm chair and knitting, next to which, an old wireless radio the size of a fridge was chatting away to itself. She took hold of a large jug, reached up high to a barrel tilted on a shelf and turned the tap. Beer poured forth from a height and she moved the jug up and down, to create a head, swirling it around. Then she took two-pint pots and filled them from the jug. Walking over to them, she smiled again.

"Two and six, love." She put the glasses onto a thin shelf at the side of her door and Roger handed over two coins, which she stuffed away quickly in her pinny pocket. Sid leant to his ear.

"Give her another to put her teeth in." He whispered. Roger smiled.

"Thank you love." He lifted the two pints and ushered Sid into the back bar, who was reluctant to move further in, to say the least.

They walked into a back snug and drew a curtain behind themselves. The walls were thick, glossed anaglypta that was stained yellow by years of nicotine and the seat covers were ripped and stained too. High wooden back to the seats blocked out most of the summer evening light, what wasn't blocked was dissipated by stained blown glass in small squares, different patterns and shapes. The air was heavy with stale smoke which the two of them refreshed by lighting up two Capstan straight away. Roger blew out a heavy breath of cigarette smoke before talking.

"Just drink your drink and don't panic. We'll have one here then go and surprise them next door."

"I'm just wondering, mate, why are we waiting?" Sid flicked the ash from his cigarette nervously.

"Because" Roger blew more out. "We are the men in charge and we can take our time."

"I don't want to." Sid puffed nervously on his cigarette. "I just want to get this done."

"And we will, mate, patience." He gulped his pint before lighting another cigarette.

The curtain to their snug rattled open and in tottered the elderly landlady, carrying another jug of beer.

"Top-up, loves?" Without waiting for a reply, she re-filled their glasses, slopping it over the table, causing them both to jump back in a bid to protect their clothes and shoes. "That'll be two and six." She stood with her hand out, waiting for the money. Sid and Roger looked at each other until Sid handed over a coin again, which she shoved into her pinny and moved away a lot faster than she came.

Sid looked at Roger aghast. Two more pints? Roger smiled at him weakly.

"Another one won't hurt, will it?" He reached over and pulled one of the glasses towards himself, then pushed the other towards Sid.

"Hurt? Can we just go and get this done?" Despite his protests, he took the glass and took a long pull from it.

"Look," Roger leant over to him and said, in a very loud whisper right into his friend's ear, "we can take our time and work up a bit of courage, can't we?" He turned his wrist and showed Sid his watch. Coughing, he said, "Anyway, it's eight now, bingo will be on. We couldn't talk to them if we tried."

"You're right." Sid let out a long breath and then drained his glass. He stood, picked up the empty glasses and moved out from around the table. "Another?"

In the concert room of the Post Office Club, Maureen and Barbara were trying to concentrate on the sheets of numbers in front of them, as the Chairman shouted out numbers. Barbara kept looking at her watch.

"Where the fuck are they?" She whispered.

"SHHHHH!" A loud rebuke came from behind her, causing most of the ladies in the room to look up from their cards, pens poised and, tutting loudly, turned back to their numbers.

Maureen looked around her, smiling apologetically for her friend who she now turned to and, shrugging her shoulders, carried on marking off numbers.

"House!" In the far corner, a cry went up followed by a headscarf bobbing up and down excitedly. A collective groan resounded around the rest of the room.

"Bollocks, I only needed a six!" Maureen threw down her pen and flopped back into the plump dralon of the seat and, folding her arms and, looking at Barbara she said, "Where the fuck are they?"

Both of them were dolled up to the nine's, hair piled high on their heads and held in place by a plethora of Kirby grips and Ellnett hairspray, their cardigans draped over their shoulders, barely covering the tightness of their tops and up-lifted bosoms. They looked almost identical except for the different pastel colours of their clothes. A lot of hard work had gone into looking this good but, the objects of their efforts were nowhere to be seen.

"Well, I'm not bloody happy." Said Maureen, her arms tightly folded under her boobs, lifting them even higher. A fact that wasn't going unnoticed by several men who were dotted around the room, unable to leave their wives at bingo time, as weren't allowed money of their own. Especially when there was a bar involved.

"No, me neither." Barbara copied her friend's body language but then unfolded her arms quickly to look again at her watch. "They said half-seven." She bent her arm around to show the face of the watch to her friend. "It's half-eight!"

"Yes, yes, I know." Maureen didn't even look at the watch; she was well aware of the time.

The wall sconces around the ornate concert roomed dimmed suddenly as the stage lights brightened. The Chairman walked on, trailing the microphone cord behind him, but tangling it in his feet, causing him to kick out and shuffle, cursing under his breath but not realising the microphone on. A few of the older ladies took sharp intakes of breath at the language, their husbands laughing at the show that was being put on.

"Testing, testing," The Chairman blew into the microphone, getting an earful of feedback in return, before coughing wildly. "Now, it's time for t'turn and we have a new lad here tonight, all the way from Newcastle so, let's put our hands together for Mickey McDonald!"

Applause rang out around the room as the house lights dimmed, the floor lights coming on, as the band started playing, two blokes on a set of drums and a piano, filling the hot air with tinkling notes and a shuffling-brush backbeat, as the turn walked onto the stage.

All eyes looked stage-wards as a firm baritone began singing along to the music, perfect pitch and tone, bring to life a Perry Como number, much to the delight of the old dears in the front rows, as he launched into "A – You're Adorable"

Maureen was looking intently at her watch, trying to make out the time in the darkness, when Barbara nudged her hard in the ribs.

"Eh! Listen to this lad, 'Reen. Not a bad looker neither."
Barbara was leaning forward, watching intently, tapping
her toe along to the beat.

Maureen condescended to look up at that point, with a sigh
at her watch and cursing Roger for being so late. At the
precise moment she looked up towards the stage, she saw
the act and recognised the lad from the factory, the
electrician that was lost at lunch-time. She was amazed at
how dapper he looked, changed from his overalls, into a
fitted tuxedo, his long legs encased in tailored trousers, the
shine on his shoes, reflecting the light that shone down on
him, creating a halo-like effect from the Brylcreem on his
hair.

He saw her too, at precisely the same moment.

Smiling, he directed the lyrics of the song towards her,
never moving his eyes from hers.

The music was humming and his voice was mesmerising, as
Maureen barely blinked as she looked at him. Barbara
nudged her in the ribs gently, trying to get her attention.

"Eh 'Reen, where have I seen him before?" Barbara looked
at her friend and clicked her fingers before her eyes.

"'Reen!" She hissed louder, straight down her ear.

"Yeah? What?" Maureen answered, still not taking her eyes
off Mickey, whilst she absent-mindedly took a cigarette
from her holder and promptly lit the filter end. "Pfft! Pfft!"
She spat quickly, the acrid taste filling her mouth before
trying to regain her composure. Barbara shoved a hanky to
her face and blotted her friend's lips, smudging her lipstick
at the corners, making her look sad all of a sudden. "Thank
you, thank you" Maureen pushed the hanky away before
looking back towards Mickey, who was nearing the end of

the song gearing up for a finale. Barbara put her hand against Maureen's back and pushed firmly.

"Toilets" She hissed, "Now."

"No! He's doing a big finish!"

Barbara tried to tug her arm but Maureen wasn't moving. Mickey stepped off the stage, to a series of 'ahh's' from the older women along the front of the stage but Mickey kept his eyes on Maureen, singing to her. He stepped closer. Once, twice, his long strides walking across the dance floor and then, he was between tables, pulling his cable along with him, singing all the way, a crescendo building. He got within four feet of Maureen, and, pointing his fingers, gestured her to come and join him as he finished his number.

Barbara tightened her grip on her friend's arm, determined to not let her move from the seat but, as if by an unseen power, Maureen rose, looking Mickey straight in the eyes and, not blinking, held her hand out to him. Barbara's hand flopped to the velvet seat, vacant.

Mickey and Maureen's hands were so close, almost touching as he took a step forward but suddenly, the cable of his microphone was taught, and he snapped back suddenly, whisking his hand away from hers. Maureen was stood up in a seated room, her arm raised, fingers outstretched with Mickey trying to look nonchalant at the couple of steps he'd had to stagger back under pressure from the microphone cable. He started back-stepping, never taking his eyes off Maureen's and, as he hit the last note, he raised his arm in the air, brought it down and, with a final movement, pointed back to Maureen.

The crowd erupted in applause and cheers, mainly women's, and Mickey mouthed the words: 'Drink?'

Maureen blushed, looked around the room, then looked back to him, nodding emphatically.

She turned and sat back down to the stoic look of Barbara who, legs crossed and arms folded, blew smoke at her and shook her head.

"What?" Asked Maureen innocently.

"You know very well what."

"I'm only having a drink with him" She avoided all eye contact and took a compact from her bag. Seeing the mess that Barbara had made of her lipstick, she made a little yelp and ran head long into the toilets. She passed Dennis, Roger's friend, who was sitting at the door with the raffle tickets, the loose ones in his hands ruffling to the floor as she created a breeze with her speed.

"Eh! You didn't have the meat pie, did you?" He stooped to the carpet to pick everything up. "I had one of 'em" He muttered, returning to his seat, holding his stomach.

In the toilets, Maureen was applying fresh lipstick as Barbara walked in behind her, a tight look and thin lips, Maureen finally met her gaze in the mirror.

"It's just a frigging drink Babs'" She said, lips pursed against her teeth as she glossed over again.

"And what about Roger? You two are together. What would he say?" Her arms were still folded under her bosom. Maureen's Mum had always said Barbara looked like a Fish-Wife. She could have been right. Maureen sighed, put the top back on her lippy and threw it into her bag. Turning to look at her friend, she looked her square in the eye.

"And where is he, Maureen? Eh? Where's the pair of them?" She asked. Maureen didn't answer, her eyes moving from left to right. "No, you don't bloody know either!"

An elderly woman walked in at that point, picked up the vibe in a split second and dived straight into the nearest cubicle.

Maureen dropped her voice to a pseudo-whisper.

"I'll tell you where they are, on this supposedly 'big' night of ours, pissed up somewhere, trying to get some Dutch bloody courage. We knew what was coming tonight – the big proposal – two mates and their birds, all happy together! Christ!" She turned back to the mirror and adjusted her bra, her back to Barbara but her head at ninety-degrees, still looking at the expression on her face, which was now slightly contrite. She turned to face her. "Look, they're not here, we are."

"I know 'Reen but, please, a drink with another fella?" Barbara's arms had fallen to her sides, beseeching her friend.

"It's just a drink, Babs'. I recognise him from work. A contractor. He'll be no bother."

"But Roger!" Pleaded Barbara as Maureen went to open the door. She paused and looked back at her friend.

"He's left me waiting for the last time, Babs'. Fuck him!"

"Eh!" A reedy voice piped up from the cubicle. "No need for that language in here!"

"Oh, shit-off!" Cried Maureen, and she strode back into the club, looking for Mickey.

"Sho, we'll just have one more and then we'll go next door." Roger slurred, lifted his pint and drained the dregs into his mouth. He got no response from Sid, who was slightly slumped in the corner, eyes half closed. Sid slowly opened them, felt a wave of nausea and moved forward, inhaling deeply.

"No" Sid struggled to sit up straight, "Letsh go now, I won't make no sense if we have another." He sat up but his shoulders were hunched. He tried to focus on his friend but needed to shut one eye to do it.

"Ah, mebbe you're right." He stood, swayed, before sitting back down suddenly, his balance gone. "Oops! Try again." He gripped the edge of the table this time, his fingertips squeaking against the beaten copper top, sliding when they hit a pond of beer spillage. "Come on. Let's do it." He stood more slowly this time, knees bent, before rising into a full stand. He turned around to Sid, who was struggling. Holding out his hand to lift him, he laughed, "They'll be wondering where we are!"

Maureen and Mickey were sitting in the snug, knees touching and giggling softly. Maureen raised her drink to her lips and demurely took a sip. Mickey smiled at her.

"I've been thinking about you all day, you know." Mickey moved his glass around, swirling the contents of a scotch, before sipping gently at the rim.

"Liar," she said, thinking how sophisticated he looked, sipping his drink, and not gulping pints like Roger. Then she realised it was the first time she'd thought about Roger in over an hour. She shook the thought of him from her head. "You've not thought about me since this morning. Once you found the canteen, I was gone!"

"Ah, that's not true, pet." His soft lilting Geordie accent warmed her, "I've thought of nowt else."

"Really?" She looked up at him, her eyelids low, "Do you mean that?" Mickey reached across to take her hand and she felt her finger tips touch his. A wave of electricity went through her.

"Aye, I do."

A sudden commotion washed through the bar, causing Mickey and Maureen to raise their heads. She heard Roger's voice loudly greeting people in the club, Sid's too.

"Oh fuck." She whispered. She snapped her hand out of Mickey's.

"What is it?" He asked.

"Trouble." She replied.

"Hello Roger, Sid!" She heard Barbara loudly announcing their presence, for the benefit of Maureen in the snug. "What kept you?"

"Baby!" Sid shouted in reply. "I'm here!" Maureen heard a tussle; no doubt Sid had grabbed her and she was having none of it.

"You're pissed!" Barbara cried. Maureen groaned inwardly, hearing Barbara's voice. Pissed up, this would be ten times worse. Suddenly, she saw Roger looming over the table, staring at the scene before him, swaying unsteadily on his feet.

"What's all this?" He cried, pointing at Mickey but looking at Maureen.

"Who's this?" Asked Mickey. Maureen looked between them, wondering who to respond to first.

"Roger!" She tried to smile and speak softly, "where have you been? I was getting worried."

"Never mind that." He snarled." I asked you who the fuck is this?"

"Ey, there's no need for that, lad." Mickey had turned in his seat. He quickly summed up the situation. Turning to Maureen, he smiled. "Oh, is this the boyfriend you've been telling me about?" He turned back to Roger. "You're a lucky man. She's done nothing but talk about you all night." He smiled at Roger, trying to diffuse the atmosphere.

"Shut up. I wasn't asking you." Roger had his arms by his sides, hands balling to fists.

"Roger! Shhh! You're drunk. Let's go outside, get some fresh air." She reached out to catch his arm, which he quickly snapped away. A crowd had gathered, watching the scene unfold before them.

"Aye, that'll be the best thing, lad" Mickey was still trying to calm the situation.

"I'm not your lad and the only person I'm going outside with is you." He tried to poke Mickey in the chest but missed.

"Roger!" Hissed Maureen.

"And you can shut up, tart!" He snarled and took a step towards Maureen, at which point, Mickey stood and raised himself to his full height, slowly. Roger's gaze followed his until he realised he was now looking up at the man he was offering outside.

Mickey's demeanour quickly changed and, putting his face close to Roger's, he snarled back. "You do not talk to a lady like that!" He turned to Maureen, smiled and winked.

"Don't worry pet, he'll sober up in the fresh air. He turned back to Roger. "Outside. Now."

Mickey strode past Roger, knocking his shoulder, causing him to stagger a bit more than he already was. He puffed up his chest and followed, striding after the tall Geordie towards the front doors. Maureen went after them, followed by Barbara and Sid, who was looking dumb-struck and a little green around the gills.

There was a pause in the club. They watched silently as the small group moved outside. After a few glances at each other they moved, as a body, as the whole club rushed to the door in a bid to get outside to see what was going on. Out beside the road, Mickey stood waiting on the grassed verge that sat beneath the stone city walls, where a few curious pigeons looked on.

Roger removed his sports coat as if to show he meant business. He held it out to Maureen behind him to hold but she just folded her arms, not believing this was happening. Sid stepped forward.

"I've got this mate." He took the jacket and stepped a safe distance away, hoping he wouldn't have to step in any further.

The crowd that spilled out onto the pavement, spread itself along the length of the club, some had brought out beer crates to stand on to get a better look. A few of the older clientele were stood on the seats inside, peering from the windows, the net curtains pushed wide, they're eyes flicking from left to right, watching the scene unfold.

Mickey held out his hands, palms up and leant forward. "This doesn't have to go any further. Just apologise to the lady and we'll call it quits."

"Scared are ya?" Roger sneered at him, his hands balled into fists and he smiled at the ripple of laughter that came from the crowd behind him. He felt suddenly confident, knowing he was on home turf.

He shuffled his feet, and started moving towards Mickey who, in response, moved to the side, and brought his hands up but kept them loose, as the two of them began circling each other, slowly.

"Go on Roger!" Sid called out, "Knock the twat out!"

The tension became palpable as Mickey and Roger moved around each other. Roger weaved a bit, to try and show off to Maureen who still stood with her arms folded, scowling at him. The crowd was added to by the regulars of the other pubs on the street, who stood watching, pint glasses in hand, lighting cigarettes, with a general murmur of conversation about the scene before their eyes.

Suddenly, Roger lunged forward, trying to throw a punch but only grabbing the lapel of Mickey's jacket, tearing out the carnation he had in his button hole. Mickey merely stepped to the side and watched as Roger tried to regain balance. Roger spun around and went to launch again. This time, as his punch whistled past Mickey's ear, a sharp uppercut connected with Roger's stomach as Mickey side-stepped and, bringing his arm back, he quickly back-handed him across his left ear, before stepping back to clear some space. Roger folded like paper, the wind knocked from him and his ear ringing from the slap, he descended to the ground, trying to draw breath before throwing up the evening's drink, all across his trousers, all across the road, The crowd gave a collective 'urggh' at the sight of him crumpled in the road, covered in sick and trying to breathe desperately.

Mickey stepped over to where his carnation lay on the ground and, brushing it off, he pulled it through into the button hole. He looked over to where Maureen stood, mouth open and shrugged at her, an apologetic look on his face.

He began walking up the road, away from the crowd, knowing he would be the least popular person in York tonight. It took him a monumental effort not the look back. Maureen looked at Roger, still gasping for air on his knees and then looked towards the retreating back of Mickey, his long legs striding out, heading towards the main road. "Mickey! Wait!" She called after him and began to trot up the hill towards him. Roger stopped gasping long enough to watch her going up the hill towards the man who had just floored him, before the need for oxygen took over and he began trying to inhale again.

The crowd began melting away, disappointed that the entertainment for the evening was over. The fight had lasted seconds and now the night's turn was wandering towards the city centre. Muttering between themselves, they went back into the club and their respective pubs, leaving Roger kneeling on the road, the only people still with him were Sid and Barbara. Sid's face was green after looking at the sick on the road and Barbara looking furious at both of them.

"Well, I hope you're both happy!" She cried, turned on her heel, and went back into the club.

Sid watched her go, turned to his friend and bent down to pick him up. Using Roger's new sports coat to wipe the vomit off his trousers, he tucked his arms under Roger's armpits and heaved him up onto his feet. Roger looked at Sid, disbelief in his eyes.

"What just happened?"

Chapter Twenty-three
A Hard Act to Follow
1958

"Mickey!" Maureen called after him as he rounded the corner, into Exhibition Square. He stopped in front of the fountain, the water jets tinkling water into a small pond of green water into which he looked, his shoulders moving up and down as he breathed deeply. She walked up behind him and put a hand on his shoulder.

"I'm sorry, pet." He said, not looking at her. "I hate fighting but I hate men speaking to lasses like that even worse." Turning him around, Maureen could see his eyes were red and he was frowning, not in anger, she could see that, but in disappointment.

"It's not your fault, Mickey. He was drunk. He's not normally like that."

"No excuse that, either." He touched her hand and she responded to the pressure of his grip. "Drunks are no good, you know. I had one for a father and he treated me mam awful."

"So that's why you hit him?" She smiled sarcastically at him, trying to lighten the mood.

"Aye." He laughed. "That and he was being a twat."

"Well, I can't argue with you there." She laughed too, still holding his hand.

"Is he always like that?" Asked Mickey, his smile turning slightly. "'Cos if he is, you mebbe should reconsider seeing the fella."

Barbara shook her head, smiling and looked down. "No, he's not like that. I think him and Sid were going to pop the question tonight to me and Barbara. I think the Dutch courage went a bit too far."

"Married! To him!" He barked a laugh and then saw the sad reaction on her face. "I'm sorry pet. I didn't mean that. Sorry."

"It's ok." She looked back into his eyes and saw genuine remorse. "You'd just have to get to know him better, that's all."

"I don't think there's any chance of that, do you?"

"No, I doubt it too." They both laughed now, the mood lightened. Mickey looked about the square, trying to orientate himself. He knew little of York except the factory and his digs for the night.

"Well, I don't think I'll be welcome back at that club, do you?" He said. "Do you want to go back? See how he his?" Barbara thought for a moment.

"No, he's ruined the night. Sod him."

"Well, I'm off for a drink then." He paused, smiled at her and asked, "Would you care to join me?"

"I'd love to." She replied without hesitation and, linking her arm through his, they walked toward the centre and as far from the working men's club as possible.

The next morning, Maureen woke with a start to a hammering at her door. Her head was banging and it took her a few seconds to realise she was at home, in bed. She looked around herself and saw a small piece of paper and a pink carnation laid on the pillow next to her. In a flash, it all came back to her, the night on the town with Mickey, lots of drinks and then the stumbling walk home. With him.
Oh God, she thought.

She grabbed the piece of paper and unfolded it. It took a few seconds for her eyes to focus before she could read the few scrawled lines.

Maureen,

Thank you for making a bad night into one of the best I've ever had. I hope you can make it alright with your fella and I wish you all the best for the future.

I'm going back to Newcastle today, so I doubt I'll ever see you again but you're a special lady, so make sure he treats you like one.

Love, Mickey

Oh God, she thought again.

She heard footsteps on the landing and her housemate's voice, closely followed by Roger's. She grabbed the note and flower and shoved them under her bed and then heard a tentative knock at the door.

"Maureen?" She heard Roger's muffled and apologetic voice from behind the wood. "Are you there, Maureen?"

"Yes" she croaked in response, cleared her throat and repeated, "Yes, I'm here."

"Can I come in?" His voice had taken on a whining tone, so Maureen climbed out of bed, straightened the covers and walked to the door. Opening it, she saw Roger's eyes above a large bouquet of flowers, his eyebrows raised in anticipation of having to do a lot of grovelling for the night before but, instead, he got her arms thrown around him, crushing the flowers against his chest, before she pulled him into her room, ignoring the disapproving look from her housemate.

Roger was stunned. He wasn't expecting this.

"I'm sorry about last night, love. I'd had too much to drink and it was a shock, you know, to see you talking with another bloke." He babbled the words out, having practised them a thousand times already.

"Don't be daft," Maureen took the flowers from him and straightened them out, not looking him in the eye. "These things happen."

"I'm blaming Sid, you know. He kept saying 'have another' when all I wanted to do was come to you." Roger had regained some of his bravado as he watched Maureen fussing around the room, looking for somewhere to lay the flowers whilst, at the same time, she kicked discarded clothes and underwear under the bed, hoping he wouldn't notice.

He did notice however, that she wouldn't sit down.

"Are you alright?" He asked.

"Me? What? Yes, why wouldn't I be?" She stammered, turning her back to her dresser and looking at him. "Don't I look alright?"

"Well, can I sit down?" he moved over to the bed.

"Yes, yes, of course." She didn't move but her eyes lit on the carnation underneath that she hadn't quite pushed far enough in, out of sight. She rushed to sit next to Roger, so he wouldn't stand up.

"I just wanted to say I'm sorry for being an idiot, Maureen. It won't happen again, I promise." He put his arm around her and pulled her into him. She relaxed slightly and let herself rest into his shoulder.

"It was embarrassing Roger. We'd planned for a big night and it was ruined after what you did."

"I know, I know. It was stupid." He stood up from the bed and Maureen immediately stiffened as he turned to look back.

Please don't see the flower, please don't see the flower, she whispered to herself.

"If you two hadn't stormed off, I'd have apologised."

"Which two? Who?" She snapped back to attention.

"Well, you and that Mickey. I saw you following him up the street. Your soft, you are." Roger was smiling down at her now.

"What do you mean?"

"Well, running to apologise to him. For me. There was no need to do that." He moved closer to Maureen and took her hand.

"Oh, well, you know, I felt bad for the bloke. He'd only been singing a few songs and that happened." She sighed inwardly with relief at the way the conversation was turning.

"And my green-eyed monster reared its ugly head." Roger tutted at himself. "I am sorry and I'll tell him when I see him. Buy him a drink and shake his hand."

"You can't; he's gone." She said quickly, then winced, regretting it.

"Gone? Where?" Roger's tone changed to one of doubt. "How would you know?"

"Er, he said that he was going home, you know, while I was apologising. For you." Maureen was twisting the hem of her nightdress as she spoke, wishing to God she was anywhere but there, right now.

"Oh, right." Roger paused, his mind whirring, watching the hem of the night dress get more twisted as Maureen fidgeted.

Something was wrong. Could she still be angry with him or was it something else?

"Well, seeing as I'm here, I've something to ask you." He reached into his pocket and pulled out a jeweller's box and, spinning around, he went onto one knee.

Oh God, she thought, not on the floor, no.

He flipped the cover open and there, glinting in the light, was a diamond engagement ring.

"Maureen. Would you do me the honour of being my wife?" He said, solemnly.

She grabbed his wrists and lifted him from the floor, so quickly, he stumbled into her.

"Yes! Yes, I will!" She kissed him forcefully, taking his breath away and also taking his gaze from anywhere except the flower on the carpet, poking out from under the bed.

He stumbled back, stunned but grinning and happy. He grabbed her and hugged her, leaning in for a more affirming kiss but she put her hand to his chest and leaned back.

"Now, why don't you go and wait for me in the living room and I'll get washed and dressed." She gently pushed him towards the door. "Maybe we can go and celebrate? Get a bite to eat? I'm starving."

"Oh, yes, ok. That sounds great." He still looked slightly stunned. He hadn't expected it to be this easy. He was just engaged and was being shoved out of the door. "I'll go and have a smoke and wait for you then."

"Yes, you do that, I'll not be long." She pushed him from the room and, grabbing her dressing gown, she followed him, pulling the door closed behind her, with a resounding 'click'.

She watched him walk down the stairs. He got to the bottom and turned to look back at her watching him. She waved delicately, smiling. He waved back and stepped into the living room.

On the landing, Maureen breathed out a massive sigh of relief. Jesus, she thought, that was close, before heading into the bathroom to wash off last night and all that might have happened. If only she could remember.

Downstairs, Roger made himself comfortable in one of the armchairs and, reaching for yesterday's newspaper, he settled down to wait. He delved into his pocket for his cigarettes and then began shifting about, looking for his lighter.

Nothing.

He stood and looked around the room for a lighter or a box of matches, anything, but there was nothing. A house full of factory girls kept the place immaculate.

He put the paper back on the coffee table and went back upstairs to see if he could find a lighter in Maureen's room. He heard her splashing water around in the bathroom and softly opened her door and crept in.

He looked on top of her dresser; nothing. He lifted her handbag from the floor and rummaged around until he found a box of matches at the bottom. Bingo, he thought. Striking one, he looked at the end of his cigarette as he lifted the flame nearer and there, on the floor, poking out from under the bed, was a slightly crushed pink carnation. Just like the one Mickey had been wearing in his button hole last night. He stopped breathing. Right until the flame on the match reached his fingertips.

"Arrgh!" he flapped his arm around to extinguish the flame before continuing to stare at the flower. "What the bloody hell…" He muttered to himself.

He bent down to retrieve it but then he heard the water stop in the bathroom so he darted for the door and ran down the stairs, listening for Maureen's footsteps on the floor above. As he listened to the padding of her feet, his mind went into overdrive and began picking over what he had seen. It can't be. Him? In her room? No, he'd just given her the flower. But why had she kept it? In her room? His mind went into overdrive.

With some force, he struck another match and lit his cigarette, ruminating over what he had just seen.

"Roger! I'm ready!" Maureen called from the top step. Stepping onto the hallway, he looked up and saw her all made up, her coat and bag over her arm, ready to go. She was smiling down at him, obviously happy that it was him she was going to town with. He smiled back. She was beautiful. And she was his.

She certainly wasn't some lanky Geordie streak-of-piss' girl; that was for sure.

He'd won.

He'd ask her about the flower another time.

"Ready when you are, love." He said softly, deciding to put the flower to the back of his mind.

Chapter Twenty-four
The Confession
Bridlington 1978

"*… I'm going back to Newcastle today, so I doubt I'll ever see you again but you're a special lady, so make sure he treats you like one.*

Love, Mickey"

Barbara's lips moved over the words as she read the dog-eared note that Maureen had passed her, the folds slightly brown from years of being tucked away in her purse, in a pocket Roger would never know was there.

"Wow." Said Barbara. "And you never saw him again until last night?" Her face was slightly incredulous, her eyes narrowed slightly. Maureen snatched the note back off her.

"Of course, I bloody didn't. I was married two months later." She busied herself re-folding it and carefully slotting it back in the folds of her purse.

"Married. Hmm." Barbara leant back in her seat; arms folded.

They were now sitting in the small bar of the Grand Hotel, the windows facing the beach, where they could see the holiday makers having a good time. They were sipping halves of lager, trying to eliminate the residual hangovers whilst around them, a few residents were gathering, waiting for their evening meal to be served.

"What does 'hmm' mean?" Maureen asked defensively.

"Married: expecting." Barbara was smiling knowingly.

"Yes, well, isn't that what happens most of the time? Almost everyone we know was up the spout when they walked down the aisle, otherwise they wouldn't have bloody gone down it!"

"And Michael was born, when? Remind me."

"You bloody well know when Michael was born, you're his frigging Godmother!" Maureen was getting increasingly uncomfortable now.

Barbara leaned forward and took hold of Maureen's hands between her own.

"Look, I'm not accusing you of nothing. You said yourself that he was with you for one night but you've been with Roger forever, so what are the odds of Michael not being Roger's?"

Maureen looked shocked at Barbara voicing something that she had held in her head for years.

"Barbara, listen, that note is the only memory I have of that night. I don't remember anything except waking up and finding that note." Small tears began running down Maureen's face as Barbara gripped her hands more tightly.

"We went out on the town after the fight outside the club. I was angry with Roger for ruining that night, angry and upset but Mickey well, he just made everything alright." Barbara's eyebrows rose again. "No, I didn't mean THAT!"

"Ok, alright." Barbara soothed.

"At least, I don't think I do…" She paused, trying hard to remember.

"He must have made sure I got home safely; that's all I know and I'm grateful to him for that but I don't know how long he stayed or when he left; that's the thing."

"So, what happened next?" Barbara asked.

"Roger showed up with flowers to apologise. Asked me to marry him." She looked up into her friend's eyes. "I said yes, just to get him off the scent of anything being wrong."

Barbara patted her hands in understanding. "I realised that Mickey was just a passing thing. Roger was real; stable."

"And then?" Barbara took a sip of her drink, the lager going down a bit more easily now.

"Roger stayed that night and the three nights after."

"You made sure there was no confusion then?" Barbara put her glass back on the table and leaned back in.

"It wasn't just that, it was to reassure him. He'd been a bit strange with me after that night, as though he wasn't sure about me. I wanted him to know getting married was the right thing to do." Maureen grabbed another napkin from the dispenser on the table, the pile of wet paper building between them both. She blew her nose.

"And then?" Barbara asked.

Maureen just set her lips and raised her eyebrows.

"Oh right. Michael." Barbara leant back again.

"A month later, we found out I was expecting and we brought the date forward." Maureen sighed and sat back in the chair and gazed out to sea. The evening sun was changing the colour of everything, the people on the beach had thinned out and a few were still packing up. Where were her boys now, she wondered? Barbara followed her gaze.

"It's getting late and we've been out all day. The lads'll be wondering where we are."

"I wonder what state they're in." Maureen stated it; it wasn't a question. They both knew that Roger and Sid would've been in a pub all day, probably well into their cups by now. Barbara sighed.

"Come on, I'm starving. My treat." She stood up and drained her drink with a satisfied smack of the lips. "Let's get some chips and take a slow walk back." She held out her hand and Maureen took it, lifting herself out of the chair. "And then we'll go and find them."

"Yes, I suppose you're right." She paused as they stood at the doors to the bar. "Might as well get it over with." They both reached into their purses and pulled out sunglasses and, putting them on, they went down the stairs to the pavement linking arms, as they began walking towards the south beach front.

They walked against the flow of pedestrians who were heading back to digs or campsites, carrying bags from the beach, looking red, hot and tired. Maureen noticed a few were limping and one bloke had a nasty bruise on his cheek and wondered if there'd been a fight. She heard a few mutterings and the word 'bulldog'.

Fighting. She was sick of it. Men!

They crossed the road by the harbour and stopped at a small chippy to grab some food. They took their newspaper wrapped parcels, shuffling them around in their hands so as not to burn themselves and slowly walked towards the end of the harbour wall, neither saying anything before they sat and unwrapped their chips. The smell of hot fat and vinegar hit them and they both realised they hadn't eaten all day. Barbara passed Maureen a small wooden fork and they dug in.

"There's one thing that's been bothering me though." Barbara said, as she tried spearing scraps of batter onto a chip.

"What's that?" Maureen paused, chip to mouth.

"Why did you call him Michael? Didn't that make it obvious?"

Maureen put her chip-laden fork back down and stared at her friend who was slowly chewing a chip.

At precisely the same time, their faces cracked into smiles, then into gales of laughter. Barbara's half-chewed chip on full display, unable to keep control.

"Ah, bloody hell! That was Roger's idea!"

"Roger's?" Barbara was coughing now, "How come?"

"His Dad was called Michael!" Maureen was struggling to keep hold of her chips, she was laughing that hard. "Of all the names! Christ!"

Chapter Twenty-five
Have you seen her?

Slim strode gingerly over the sand, his ankle swollen and hurting, shifting the box of beer onto his other hip, trying to relieve the pressure on his bruised ribs. Behind him, Nutty was limping heavily, a long graze down his thigh, leading to a bruised and swollen knee, he carried two steaming bags of fish and chips as they made their way over the dunes to where the others were laid.

As walking wounded, they had been sent on the errand, the others laid on the sand nursing sore heads and bruised hands from the game earlier.

Coming over the grassy tops, they saw that the others had barely moved, only emptied a few more cans of lager. Billy looked up when he heard them approach.

"Hey, here they are. Supper has arrived." He lifted himself up off the sand slowly, his legs aching from all the sprinting as the others started moving, groaning with the effort.

"Here you go, lads." Nutty walked into the middle of them and began handing round wrappers of food, Slim followed him and, opening the box of lager, began decanting the tins into a bucket of cold water. James hobbled over and took one from him, snapping it open and drinking thirstily.

"Cheers mate." He said, paused and burped.

"Thank you" replied Slim, wafting the fumes away with his hand.

Nutty held out a newspaper wrapped parcel to Slim who took it and sat in the sand, not opening it. The others began shovelling chips into their mouths, hungry after the day's exertions until Billy looked over to where Slim sat, his food still unopened, staring out towards the sea.

"You alright, Slim?" He called over as Slim snapped back to attention. "You not hungry?"

"Yeah, yeah no, I'm fine. Sorry, miles away then." He began unwrapping the newspaper slowly and the chips billowed a cloud of steam into his face as he just looked at them, remembering the chips he had last night with Collette.

He looked back over to the sea shore and focussed on a container ship, far out in the distance and wondered where Collette was right now and what she was doing.

He re-wrapped his food and placed it on the sand and looking around him at the others stuffing their faces, he felt a sudden desire to get back into town and look for her.

"Are we heading to town tonight?" He asked. The others looked at him in surprise.

"You in a rush, son?" Asked James, still chewing.

"Yeah, there's ages yet, it's not even seven." Michael was wiping his grease-stained paper with the last of his chips, trying to soak up all of the vinegar and salt residue.

"I was just going to start getting ready." Slim stood, picking up the food parcel and walked over to them. He dropped it back on the sand in front of Michael saying, "You can have them," and went into the tent, leaving them all in stunned silence. Slim had never left food before.

"What's up with him?" Nutty asked, picking up the parcel and unwrapping it. "Did he get a crack on the head today, or what?"

"It's that lass, isn't it. The one he met last night?" Michael leaned forward and grabbed a handful of the chips and dropped them into his own paper.

"Do you think?" Nutty moved the wrapper, guarding against anymore handfuls being taken. "Must be bad for him to be off his food."

"Love sick, I'd say. Give me some chips then!" James reached forward to grab a handful.

"Ah leave him alone, you lot." Billy screwed up his own wrapper and stood to follow Slim into the tent while the others watched him go.

"Don't you want some chips?" Nutty called after him, and, receiving no response, just shrugged and let James take a handful, keeping the rest for himself.

Billy leaned in through the flap of heavy canvas and saw Slim shaking out a clean shirt from his bag.

"You might wanna have a wash before you put that on mate. You smell a bit ripe."

Slim turned to see Billy smiling at him as he carried on shaking out the shirt. He paused and sniffed his armpit.

"You might be right." He laid the shirt out on his sleeping bag and went to pick up his wash bag.

"You ok?" Asked Billy, "You've not eaten, it's not like you." Slim let his shoulders drop and looked at the roof of the tent.

"Look, let's have a night off the Slim jokes, can we? I just want to go out and not lay on the sand all night getting pissed with you lot!"

"Hey, easy son." Billy soothed, "I'm just concerned about you, that's all. You're not yourself."

Slim relaxed and looked at his friend who was already looking tanned and even more handsome.

"No, I know. I just can't stop thinking about her, that's all." He took his razor and some soap from his bag and shuffled, embarrassed, from foot to foot. Billy smiled at him and reached for his own wash things.

"Come on then. Bath-time." He held open the flap of the tent and beckoned Slim out. "Ignore them lot. Let's go and find this girl, eh?"

An hour later, all five of them were washed, shaved and dressed for another night on the town. Slim had borrowed some of Billy's aftershave and was feeling only marginally more confident than he had the previous night, when he had first met Collette. Billy had issued strict instructions that no piss-taking was to be directed at Slim and they all strode into town with purpose, looking for Slim's girl, whilst not ignoring the fact that they were all on a similar mission themselves.

The evening was warm again, the pubs emanating the babble of voices and the hum of music as the five walked back to the same pub they had started in the night before. It was busy as they stepped in and scanned the crowd, looking into corners and walking through into the courtyard at the back. She wasn't there.
Billy put his hand onto Slim's shoulder and shouted into his ear to be heard above the noise. "Any luck?" Slim just shook his head. In reply, Billy just tilted his head towards the door and they all left the way they had come, without buying a drink.
Outside they lined up on the pavement.
"Are we not staying, then?" Nutty asked. "I could do with a drink, me."
"There's a lot of pubs here, Slim. Let's just stick our head in a few and see if she's around." He said, ignoring Nutty.
"Yeah," said Michael, "those birds from last night weren't there either. They must spread themselves about." A couple

of girls walked past them and smiled as they went into the pub.

"Wouldn't mind that spread over me." James leered after them.

"Shut up, you. Let's go." Billy led Slim away and the others reluctantly followed him down the street to another pub on the corner.

After some more false starts, they came to a bar overlooking the harbour. They were hot, tired and thirsty, having been in almost every pub and bar in Bridlington.

The evening was getting darker now and the lights around the harbour were shining brightly as people milled around, shouting to friends and laughing. The tang of the sea air was strong and the noise from the rides and arcades washed over them, the high-pitched screams and laughter rippled through the evening.

"Right, this is it, if she's not here, I don't care. Sorry Slim but it's our holiday too and I'm gasping for a pint." Nutty strode through the doors, closely followed by Michael and James.

"Yeah, me too." Michael repeated and walked in. Slim just looked to Billy who smiled at him a little sadly.

"They're right mate. We can't spend all of our time looking for one bird in thousands. She might not even be out tonight."

"No, it's OK. I'm being too hopeful." Slim looked down, dejected. Billy took his arm.

"No, no you're not. You're showing determination. That's good." He reached out and held open the door for him. "Come on. It's not over yet."

They stepped into the darkness of the bar, feeling the throb of the juke box under their feet and made a beeline for the bar, where Nutty had already got an order in and passed around pints of cold lager. Slim took one in his hand and gazed hopefully around. Nutty chinked glasses with him, causing some lager to slop onto Slim's hand.

"Cheers! Here's to night two!" Nutty exclaimed.

Slim hardly noticed, just waved his hand to rid himself of the lager dripping through his fingers and continued looking around.

"Come on, let's go and look." Billy steered Slim away from the bar and they slowly moved around the crowd, looking in corners for Collette, Billy eager to make up for lost time by surveying the crowd for himself.

Half way around, he turned to Slim. "I don't really know who I'm looking for anyway." Only to see Slim frozen to the spot, staring straight ahead of him. Billy followed his gaze. There, in a corner, was Collette, laughing and joking with a man, whose back was turned towards them. Billy appraised the scene in a split second and turned back to his friend.

"Well, y'know…" but Slim was gone. "Ah shite." Billy whispered under his breath and went towards the doors after him. Michael called after him.

"Oi! Where you off?" He didn't get a reply.

Outside, Billy looked right and left and just saw Slim's stubby legs moving around the bar to the harbour steps alongside.

"Slim!" He called after him but Slim wasn't listening. Billy ran after him and, on getting to the bottom, could see Slim standing next to the harbour wall. The tide was out, revealing thick mud that had been washed into deep crevices, the small fishing boats listed on their sides, waiting for the water to come back in. The smell was nauseating, with crusty fishing nets and crab pots drying in the warm evening air. Slim didn't turn around but he felt Billy come up behind him on his shoulder.

"I wouldn't jump if I were you. The smell will kill you if you stand here long enough." He saw Slim's hands clenched into chubby fists. "Come on mate. It's not that bad."

"Oh, it's alright for you, isn't it? Ships that pass in the night, and all that."

"You know what I meant." Billy tried to soothe him. "We've only just got here and there's loads of time, isn't there?"

"Not for me. Never for me." Slim's voice was cracking. Billy sighed, not quite knowing what to say without upsetting him even more.

Behind them, they heard footsteps and Billy turned to look. Behind him was Collette.

With the bloke she'd been sat with.

Christ thought Billy.

"Slim?" Collette's voice caused him to turn suddenly, then Slim saw the man standing with her and frowned. "I thought I saw you come in." She added.

"Well, we have to try and see all the sights while we're here, love." Billy tried to lift the atmosphere a bit.

"Weren't you going to say hello?" She asked, ignoring Billy, her voice a little sad.

"You looked busy." Slim replied morosely

"Busy?" She asked, a look of confusion on her face.

"With your fella." Slim gestured to the man standing next to her, taking in his size, his clothes and long curly hair, styled perfectly. Everything better than his.

Collette still looked confused and turned to look at the man beside her, who in turn, looked back at her. Billy was looking at all three, his eyes darting between them, wondering where the hell this was going to end. He didn't want enemies in this town. Not so soon, anyway.

Collette began to laugh, gently at first and then the man she was with lifted his chin and laughed loudly into the evening air, revealing perfect teeth in a tanned face, which caused Collette to laugh even louder.

"Collette love, I think we've found a green-eyed monster." The man's voice was light, effeminate, as he took in Slim and Billy standing at the edge of the harbour wall, looking confused.

Billy noticed the man's eyes check him out all over before his eyes met his. He twigged straight away and smiled at them.

"What's so funny?" Asked Slim. Collette stopped laughing and looked at Slim sympathetically. Stepping towards him, she took his hand in hers and his guard immediately dropped. She turned him slightly and pointed to the man she was with, who was still smiling, his hands on his hips, standing like a model.

"Slim, let me introduce you." She led Slim over. "This is Charlie."

"Hello." He said, holding out his perfectly manicured hand. "Slim, is it?"

"He's my hairdresser." Collette patted Slim affectionately on the shoulder. "We were just catching up."

Realisation dawned on Slim's face and he smiled at Collette and then at Charlie. He thrust out his hand and grasped Charlie's with something bordering on relief, pumping his hand up and down, he felt the softness of the skin against his own, rough callouses.

"Oh God, oh hello. I'm sorry, I just, well, you know, I just thought, well I just…" He stammered, Charlie's shoulder shaking from the pressure of Slim's hand.

"It's ok, it's ok." He pulled his hand from Slim's and waggled it in the air to relieve the pressure on his own. "No problem."

He turned to Collette who was smiling at them both and decided it was time to go. "Well, I'd better be getting along, love. Early start tomorrow."

"Oh, no, let me buy you a drink. I feel stupid." Slim looked between him and Collette, Billy was just a bystander now, wishing they could all go back inside and catch some of the action before the night was total right-off.

"No, no, honestly, I have to go." Charlie looked back at the pub up on the harbour top and then back to the group. "It's not really my scene." He said, a wry smile on his face and a surreptitious glimpse at Billy. "If you know what I mean."

"I do, mate." Billy stepped forward and took hold of Slim by the elbow. "Shall we go and buy the lady a drink?"

"No, I've had enough for one night." Collette took hold of his other elbow. "Shall we go for walk?"

Slim looked between the two until Billy let go and nodded sagely at his friend. "Off you go. Have fun."

The group broke up, Charlie heading back towards the town with a wave, Collette and Slim slowly stepping away to follow the line of the harbour wall, arm in arm.

Billy watched them go, smiling, wondering if this is what it felt like to see your kids grow up and move on. He shook his head until the sound of raucous laughter carried down to him from the pub. Time to go, he thought.

Chapter Twenty-six
When the Night is Over

Maureen tried to put her key into the Yale lock of the guest house as quietly as possible, her tongue wedged between her teeth, feeling like she was seventeen again and trying not to wake her parents.

"Are you in?" Hissed Barbara behind her, slightly slurring. They had been out all day and most of the night now, putting off the moment when they would have to go back and face their husbands.

A lot more drink had been consumed and they were both slightly wobbling, make-up smeared across their faces and looking decidedly worse for wear.

The guest house still had on its door lights, casting the hanging basket in a radiant shine as the rest of the street was cloaked in darkness, only the street lamps creating pools on the pavement. It was silent out on the street, only making their own shuffling feet and whispers sound louder.

The door clicked open and Maureen looked back with triumph.

"Yeah." She hissed as she stepped forward only to be faced Sid standing on the doormat, his arms folded across his chest.

Maureen and Barbara stood up straight, trying not to wobble, shoulder to shoulder to support each other.

"And where do you think you've been? Hm?" He sniffed the air in front of them. "And you're pissed!"

Maureen looked at Barbara and they both descended into fits of laughter.

"Ah Sid," snorted Maureen, "You sound like me Mam." She batted his folded arms as Barbara gasped for breath between fits of laughter.

"Shhh!" He looked nervously behind him, "you'll have the landlady out in a minute."

He reached out to grab Barbara who, in turn, held onto Maureen and pulled them through into the hallway.

"Upstairs now!" He shoved them towards the foot of the stairs, Barbara stumbling forward, still laughing as he got his hands on her backside and moved her, step by step, towards the landing.

"Oh Sid, you old romantic." She laughed.

"Just move now, the pair of you." He got them to the top of the landing and, before swivelling Barbara to their door, he stopped Maureen at hers. "Maureen, love, go easy on him. He's not finding this easy you know."

"Finding what easy?" She straightened up; the laughter gone from her face. "He's the one who embarrassed me by fighting in that club." She jabbed a finger in Sid's chest. "Go easy? You don't know nowt Sid, so keep your trap shut!"

Sid gripped her finger and moved it away from his chest before encircling her hand in his own, softly.

"He told me all about it, love." He smiled sadly. Maureen frowned.

"Told you what?" She was slightly afraid now, wondering what the two men had been saying to each other. She could only imagine. The words separation and divorce tumbled in her mind.

"He's had a lot to drink today and he told me about you and Mickey." He paused. "And young Michael."

"Mickey?" She cried, "Michael? What about them?"

"Shh. You don't want everyone woken now, do you?"

"I want to know what the hell you two have been saying."
She had sobered up significantly and was staring hard at
Sid. He moved back a pace.

"About what happened all those years ago, after the fight at
the club. You know, you going home with Mickey." He
reached out to lay a reassuring arm on hers but thought
better of it and drew it back. Maureen was stunned. How
the hell did he know about that? Shit, she thought.

"But, I didn't, well, not like that, no…" She was stammering
now. She looked into Sid's eyes, slightly pleading, tears
pricking the corners. "It's not true." She whispered, trying
to convince herself as much as Sid.

Sid sighed and smiled again at her in sympathy, as though
someone had died.

"It'll all come out in the wash, won't it, love."

Maureen was speechless. Sid turned back to his own
bedroom door. "We'll see you in the morning. Goodnight."
With that, he opened his door and she heard Barbara
giggling inside before Sid said, "right you…" and the door
snapped shut behind him.

Oh Christ, she thought. What the hell was happening?

She gripped the handle to their room, wondered briefly if
she had enough money for a taxi back to York rather than
face this.

No, she thought, time to face it.

She inhaled deeply, pushed the door open and stepped
inside.

The room was in semi-darkness, only a small bedside lamp
was switched on, partially illuminating Roger laid on the
bed. He had a damp flannel over his forehead and eyes and
was breathing deeply, as if asleep. Maureen breathed out in
relief. She sat gently on the side of the bed and leant down

to undo the buckle on the side of her sandals, trying not to wake him.

"'Reen?" Roger croaked. He turned his head, lifting one corner of the flannel to look at her.

"Yes Rog?" She turned to look at him. He was in a dreadful state. His hair was tousled and he hadn't shaved properly. To make matters worse, the black-eye that Mickey had given him the night before was in full technicolour.

"Are you OK 'Reen?" He reached out a hand towards her. "I'm sorry about last night love, really I am." A tear rolled down his cheek. Maureen filled up too.

"I'm alright, yes and I'm sorry too." She reached out to grasp his hand and held it. Tight.

"It was just like all those years had rolled back last night and there he was. Larger than life." He slurred slightly; the day's drinking having taken full effect.

"Shhh" She moved to lay on the bed next to him. "It's all over now. Forgotten."

"But it can't be forgotten, can it?" He asked, his voice full of emotion. Maureen froze.

"You what?" She asked, her voice trembling.

"That Mickey took you home that night after we fought outside the club." Roger was stumbling over his words, fighting back tiredness and upset, he flopped back on the pillows and closed his eyes. "You thought I didn't know. But I did. I knew." He let out a long sigh, exhaustion taking him.

How the hell did he know? Maureen played it out in her mind. Had someone seen Mickey leaving? She hadn't even seen him leaving for Christ's sake. Had her housemate said something? Bitch, if she had.

She looked at him and felt sorry for him all of a sudden. Twenty years of knowing something and not even asking her the truth.

"But it doesn't matter does it?" Roger mumbled again. "It doesn't matter." His low muttering snapped her attention back to what he was saying.

"No, it doesn't matter Rog." She still held his hand, willing him to sleep.

"Because," Roger was nearly whispering now, and Maureen leant over to hear what he was saying.

"Because what, love?" She whispered back to him, realising that he stank of drink but then, so did she.

"'Cos even if Mickey is Michael's father, I'm still his dad." He turned his head to the wall, his breathing deepening.

Holy shit, she thought, that's it. That's what he thought. It was like he'd listened in on every word she and Barbara had said today. Oh Christ, this was bad.

A cold ball formed in her stomach at the thought of Roger, her husband, having carried that thought around with him for twenty years. Scenarios played over in her mind. All the times she'd caught him staring at Michael as a boy, all the 'must take after you, not me' references that he'd come out with when Michael had missed the goal in football, failed his exams, fell off his bike. The looks as he got taller than Roger, his hair blonde as it got longer. Then that one time a teacher had called him Mickey at parent's evening, Roger had gone mad.

No, this wasn't good, wasn't good at all. This was devastating.

Roger snored next to her, still holding her hand. She gripped it tighter as the tears rolled down her face before beginning to sob as though her heart was breaking.

The worst thing was, she realised, she didn't know the truth herself.

Chapter Twenty-seven
A Gift That Keeps on Giving

Slim was on cloud nine. He was holding the hand of a woman he hadn't stopped thinking about since he'd met her last night. Was it only last night? He felt stunned, as if in a bubble. He knew the world was turning around him but he didn't care at all, just that he wanted to be here, now, at this very minute and for it to never end.

They'd walked the length of the south beach and back again, the sky was full of stars and they were alone, away from the front with the groups of people shouting and laughing.

They'd talked for most of the night, about their families, their friends, laughing and smiling. Occasionally there were sadder stories but they just held each other tighter. The hours passed and the voices from the front got quieter. Collette stopped walking and turned to look at him.

"Slim?" She asked, her body squared to his.

"Hmm?" He couldn't speak, only make noises of happiness.

"How long are you staying in Brid' for?" She grasped his other hand and pulled him a little closer to her.

"Er, well, we said we'd be here for the week at least. Maybe more. At least until the money runs out. Why?"

She leant forward to kiss him, her hand around the back of his head, fingers in his hair. He closed his eyes and felt the warmth and softness of her mouth against his and the intense pleasure coursing through his body as her the tip of her tongue parted his lips. He responded in kind, following her lead, excited as his nerve endings tingled as he pressed his body against hers, holding her tightly.

She broke the kiss and looked at him again, smiling.

"I'd like to see a lot more of you, if that's ok."

"Ok? Are you kidding me, I can't think of anything I'd want more in the world." Slim exclaimed, his world suddenly brighter, shinier. He'd never been so happy.

They kissed and laughed holding each other tightly. Could things get any better?

His mind raced at the thought of telling everyone about her. His parents, his friends; everyone.

Around them the sounds of the beach and the seafront drifted away, lost in the moment, it was only the two of them.

Watching them from the promenade, leaning on the railings, were the figures of Michael, James, Nutty and Billy. Billy smiled as he watched his little friend kiss the girl, knowing that was it for Slim; he'd found the one he was looking for. Part of him was slightly jealous and he couldn't work out why but, he mused to himself, overall he was happy for him, always having wondered if Slim would find love.

Next to him, he heard Nutty take a deep breath and lean over the wall as if to shout out but Billy just laid a hand on his arm to stop him. Nutty held his breath.

"Don't. Leave them. He's happy."

Nutty blew out the air and looked at Billy and saw his face was different, thoughtful; wistful almost.

"You alright Billy?" He asked.

"Yeah, why wouldn't I be?" He turned to see the three of them all looking at him. "What?" He asked, their faces all turned too him, Nutty smiling, Michael and James somewhat confused.

Billy turned back to look out to where Slim and his new girl were standing on the sand. They turned, hands entwined

and were strolling back towards the harbour, talking and laughing, Slim more animated than Billy had ever seen him in his life. He sighed and then felt a hand on his shoulder.
"Shall we go to the disco then?" It was Michael who asked.
"You lot go if you want to. I'm not bothered." Billy stood up straight and turned, looking at them, their faces surprised.
"I'm heading back. I fancy an early night." He turned and started walking along the path, heading towards their camp, leaving the three of them dumb-struck.
"An early night?" Called out Michael towards his back.
"You?" James was amazed. This was unheard of.
Billy didn't respond, just carried on walking as they stood there; stunned.
"Well, what are we going to do?" Michael asked the others.
"Why? Do you think he's ill or something?" Nutty stood behind the two brothers, watching Billy get further down the path.
"No, you daft sod." Michael turned to Nutty. "I meant are we still going to the disco?" James and Nutty looked at each other, unsure. James started shuffling his feet.
"Ah, I don't know mate. It doesn't seem the same without him." Nutty said, still looking at Billy's retreating back.
"Yeah, He's right." Said James, "It'd just be us. Doesn't seem right."
Michael stared at them, then turned to look at Billy, who was hardly discernible in the fading light anymore, before turning back to the others.
"He's a big lad, y'know. He's fine on his own." Their faces told him he was fighting a losing battle. "Ah, bloody hell." He kicked a small stone from the path down onto the beach in frustration. "Come on then. Let's go."

They didn't need another word as James and Nutty sped off down the path, to try and catch up with Billy. Michael followed.

"I didn't think I'd be going back with you two tonight!" He called after them before setting off after them all, leaving the bars and discos behind.

Chapter Twenty-eight
The Morning After

Maureen hardly slept that night, she listened to Roger snoring beside her and watched the sunrise through the curtains, her mind whirring, wondering what she should do. Her marriage depended on it.

She wondered where the boys were and thought about Michael, her wonderful, first-born and how happy they were when he was born, cementing their marriage and life together.

She looked down at Roger and felt both love and anger. How had he kept what he knew from her for all these years?

Not that she'd have had the answer then; she didn't now.

A part of her blamed him. If he hadn't got drunk that night, if he hadn't started that fight, if she hadn't gone with Mickey in her anger. If, if, if.

She rubbed her face in her hands, feeling with dismay the remnants of her makeup that she hadn't bothered to remove last night.

She climbed out of bed, as gently as she could, so as not to wake Roger and stepped to the sink in the corner. She ran the hot tap and gently put the plug in and let the sink fill while she inspected her face in the mirror. Her mascara had run from the tears and one eyelash was stuck to her cheek. Jesus, she thought, what a state.

She stopped the tap and splashed water over her face, gasping at the heat then took the bar of soap and rubbed it between her hands before roughly rubbing the lather over her face in a bid to rub some sense into herself.

Roger heard the tap going on and blinked but didn't move. He wondered what time it was and saw the light coming through the curtains and guessed it must be about seven o'clock.

Seagulls were crying outside and he heard some voices in the street below. His head was throbbing. Not the hangover he was expecting but he felt it, nonetheless.

Some good had come from Sid pulling him out of the pub and putting him to bed the day before. His tongue was rough and tasted awful, he was desperate for a drink of water but he didn't want to move and face Maureen, not until he knew what he was going to say. He needed to think. He needed to talk to Sid.

He heard the plug being pulled from the sink and the *woosh* of the water going down the plughole. He hoped it didn't signal what was happening to his marriage.

If only he hadn't got drunk that night twenty years ago, if only he hadn't got all jealous when he saw her with Mickey McDonald, if only he hadn't started that fight, she wouldn't have gone off with him. He ruminated on that last point. Mickey had taken her home; he knew. If only he had broached the subject with her twenty years ago, they wouldn't be in this situation now. If, if, if.

He closed his eyes again and thought about Michael. He knew in his heart that he was his but there was just that niggling doubt of needing to end the doubt.

His mind was made up. He would have to find Mickey McDonald and ask him for the truth.

But first he'd need to speak to Sid.

And get a glass of water.

Maureen looked at herself in the mirror, her face red and shiny where she'd scrubbed off yesterday and then glanced in the reflection to where Roger lay. He hadn't moved.

She realised she needed the loo and wondered if Babs was up yet. She needed to talk to her about what to do next. She looked herself in the eye and made up her mind. She would have to find Mickey McDonald and ask him what had happened that night. It was the only way she would be able to save her marriage.

She reached for her wash bag and stepped quietly to the door of the room. Turning the latch as silently as she could, she pulled open the door and stepped onto the corridor.

In a flash, Roger was out of bed and at the sink, running the cold tap and filling a glass. He drained in one, refilled it and drank that too then her cupped his hands and splashed cold water on his face. Looking in the mirror, he saw an unshaven, older man with a black eye looking back at him. He knew what he had to do, if he was to save his marriage.

Out on the corridor, Maureen was gingerly stepping across the landing, trying not too make the floorboards creak when the door to Barbara and Sid's room opened. Barbara's face appeared in the doorway and looked at Maureen.

"'Reen! I've been listening out for you!" She hissed and stepped out onto the landing and hugged her friend. "Did you sleep?"

"No, not much." Maureen replied, turning to look back at her own door. "I've left him asleep, quick, come into the bathroom."

They tiptoed quickly the rest of the way, went in the bathroom and locked the door behind them. Barbara hoisted her nightdress and noisily peed while Maureen put her washbag onto the side of the bath. When Barbara had finished, Maureen took her place and, flushing the loo, she went to sit on the edge of the bath, next to her friend.

"He knows, Babs." Maureen looked at her, tears welling in her eyes again.

"Knows what, love?" She put her hand on her friend's arm and rubbed.

"He knows that Mickey took me home that night and that Michael might not be his."

"Oh shit! You told him?" Barbara sounded amazed.

"No, he knew. He's always known. The pig-headed, stubborn bastard never thought to ask me about it!"

"But what would you have said? 'I don't know, Roger'" Barbara stared at her friend incredulously. Maureen thought that over and out her head in her hands.

"Oh Christ, Babs. For twenty years he's known and he's never said nowt. Can you believe it?" She groaned at the thought. "I sodding can't."

"But 'Reen love. You couldn't say anything different to put his mind at rest, could you?"

Maureen snapped her head up and looked hard at her friend before softening.

"No, you're right. I couldn't." She looked down at the floor and sighed. "I was sat looking at him all night and wondering what has been going through his head all these years? Has he just put it to the back of his mind?" She looked again at Barbara. "What do you think?"

Barbara stood and looked down at her, sighing too. She turned and put both taps on in the bath.

"I think you've got a good marriage, Maureen. He loves you, has done since primary school and he's always wanted to be married to you." She looked at the water filling the large, deep bath. "And I think you've got something worth fighting for."

"He said last night that, even of he wasn't Michael's father, he was still his dad. It broke my heart." Maureen dipped her hands in the hot water and swirled it around. Barbara just looked at her before crouching down so their eyes were level.

"Then that tells you all you need to know, love. You go back to how you were and never talk about it again." She stood, her knees cracking and poured some bubble bath into the water, watching the liquid being taken by it and turning it a light blue.

"And what were the odds of Mickey McDonald being the turn in the club the other night? Let's face it, if he hadn't been there, this wouldn't have reared its head again, would it?" She seemed satisfied with herself as she looked at Maureen, who was still swirling the water around.

"That's it then." Maureen said, with some finality.

"It is. Let's just forget about Mickey McDonald." Barbara began pulling her nightdress over her head.

"No, I meant, we find him tonight and we ask him."

"Eh?" Barbara's surprise was muffled by her night clothes.

"You and me. We go to that club, find him and ask him for the truth." Maureen stood and folded her arms as Barbara's head came out of the nightdress. She stood there, naked, an amazed look on her face.

"And what if you don't like the answer?" She asked.

"Well, at least I'll know. I can't spend the rest of my life wondering. It's not fair to Roger."

Barbara turned to hang her clothes on the back of the bedroom door before turning back to her friend.

"And then what? What if the actual truth finishes Roger off? What if you end up in the divorce courts?" She stood with her hands on her hips, looking down at Maureen who stood slowly so she was on eye level again.

"That won't happen. He says he loves me and he's been with me twenty years on the back of all this. We're stronger than that." She put her hands on her hips too as she realised that, for once, she didn't feel too sure about herself anymore. Barbara let her hands drop to her sides and sighed again.

"Alright, let's go and find Mickey bloody McDonald and ask him." She shook her head in defeat.

"Thank you Bab's, thank you so much." Maureen stood and hugged her, planting a big kiss on her cheek. Barbara just nodded and smiled. She looked at the bath, now full, then at Maureen.

"Do you wanna get in after me?"

Down the hall, Roger was tapping gently on Sid's door.

"Sid!" He hissed, "Wake up!"

The door opened a crack and a dishevelled Sid peered out.

"Oh, Rog. You feeling alright? I was fast asleep then." He yawned, mouth wide, a fog of bad breath enveloping Roger, who leaned back and coughed.

"Never mind that, I need your help." He craned his neck to look into the room to see where Barbara was.

"No, she's in the bathroom. It's OK. What help?" Sid pushed the door wider and stood back to let Roger in.

"I want to go and see Mickey McDonald. Tonight. At the club." He followed Sid into the room but kept his foot in the door, so he could hear Maureen coming back. He assumed she was talking with Barbara in the bathroom.

"What? Mickey?" He looked confused as he scratched his belly through his vest. "I don't get it."

"Look." Said Roger, getting exasperated. "Just listen. I need to sort this out and find the truth. No arguments, no fighting, just ask him, man to man."

"Ask him what?" Sid was coming around now but carried on scratching his belly.

"Ask him if, well…ask him. You know." Roger looked back on along the corridor. The bathroom door was still firmly shut, with the unmistakable fog of steam coming from beneath it.

"Ah, ask him if he and Maureen.." Sid was smiling as he spoke.

"Alright!" Snapped Roger. "Don't spell it out. We both know what we're talking about." Sid just sat on the bed and looked at him. "Are you going to help me, or not?"

"Aye, alright. But what if you don't like what he says? I don't want a night in the cells, mate." Sid stood up and moved to the window, lifting the curtain to take a peek out. "What time is it?" He asked.

"Time we were off, mate. Look, get yourself dressed and let's go, before they get out of there." He looked back towards the bathroom. "They'll be ages yet. Quick shave and we'll go." He made to go back to his own room.

"Hey, wait. Go where?" Sid dropped the curtain and looked at him.

"I dunno. What's believable?" Roger frowned, thinking. Sid shook his head and tutted. He lifted the curtain again and looked out. He could just see the sea, the morning sun gleaming across it, calm as a mill pond.

"Nice day out." He stated before looking back at Roger. "Sea is like glass." He added.

Roger stared at him a moment before a grin erupted on his face.

"Sid mate, you're a genius." He turned to go back to the room.

"Am I?" He stood holding the curtain, looking confused.

"Aye," said Roger, "you are. Let's go fishing!" He hurried back to his room, unbuttoning his pyjama top as he went. Sid was just standing looking nonplussed.

"Fishing?" He said to himself.

Chapter Twenty-nine
When Thoughts Turn to Home

Michael and James were sitting on the sand, looking out at the sea, watching Billy skimming stones on the water.

"How long has he been there, now?" James asked.

"Oh, at least an hour." Michael replied.

"You what?" Nutty asked, walking up behind them.

"Nothing, flower." Michael said and James smiled. Nutty looked out to where Billy was.

"How long has he been there?" He asked. Michael and James groaned in response and hung their heads.

"He's been funny since last night. Do you think he's sick of us already?" Nutty sat heavily in the sand next to them and opened a can of lager.

"Did you bring us one?" Asked James.

"Oh sorry, mate. I didn't think."

They were sitting down the beach, away from the tent, having been woken by the cries of seagulls and the clanking of empty cans being flicked by beaks, looking for food. The beach was slowly starting to fill further down towards the town and they could already hear the shouts and laughter of holiday makers carrying down towards them. The sea was calm with any waves just breaking gently on the sand. Billy just continued skimming stone after stone, not reacting when it went well, occasionally kicking the sand for more stones when it went wrong.

"I wonder what's bothering him?" Nutty asked.

"He won't tell us, will he? Keeps everything close to his chest." Michael scuffed the sand with his toes, picked up a stone and rubbed it in his palm, the loose sand falling down.

They heard rustling in the tent behind them and all turned to look, only to see Slim poke his head out of the tent to see where they all were. He was met with a raucous greeting.

"Ey, now then! Here he is, Casanova!" Shouted James.

"Late night was it? Come on, get yourself here and tell us all about it." Michael joined him. "And bring some beers!" He added. Slim just mouthed a half-hearted 'piss-off' and pulled his head back into the tent, leaving the three of them chuckling.

Ten minutes later, Slim wandered over, carrying three beers by the plastic ring and stood next to the three lads on the beach. He looked out to where Billy was still throwing stones and then turned to the others.

"How long has he been there?" He asked.

The three of them just grunted. Slim passed them the beers, keeping one back and started to walk out to were Billy was standing.

"See if you can find out what's wrong with him, can you?" Michael called after his back. Slim just nodded and carried on walking.

When he got level with Billy, he just stood, not wanting to make him jump, seeing how engrossed he was in his throwing. Billy acknowledged him with a nod and then threw another stone.

"Brought you a beer." Slim held out the can but Billy just looked at it and shook his head.

"It's a lovely day." Slim couldn't think of anything else to say and Billy didn't respond, so he just stood there, watching stone after stone hit the water.

"What's wrong, Billy?" Slim eventually asked, realising that he might get a mouthful of abuse in response. Surprisingly,

Billy paused, sighed and let the remaining stones fall from his hand.

"Ah, I don't know mate." He lifted his head to look at Slim, who had a worried expression on his face. "I'm alright, don't worry." He smiled weakly and decided to change the subject. "How are you getting on with that lass? Collette, was it?"

Slim grinned at the thought of her, then looked bashful.

"Yeah, good thanks. Seeing her tonight."

"That's good. Really great. I'm pleased for you." Billy looked anything but pleased.

"What is it Billy? Are you upset because I'm with her and not you lot?" He nodded back in the direction of the other three, where an argument had broken out. Billy followed his gaze. "I'm not ruining your holiday, am I?"

Billy laughed out loud and shook his head before turning to look at Slim.

"Don't be daft." He paused. "It's just…"

"Just what?"

"I don't know. It's just seeing you with her. Happy, like." He shook his head, his long curly hair bobbing before he reached up and tucked it behind his ears. "It's just something I've never had, you know?"

Slim looked confused.

"But you've had hundreds of girlfriends. I haven't."

"That's my point. I've had hundreds of girls. Jack the lad, me." He turned his body so he was facing Slim. "But, in all that time, with all of them…" He struggled to find the words.

"What is it?" Slim asked.

"Not one of them ever looked at me the way she looked at you. And I never looked at them the way you did with her." He paused and sighed. "Does that make sense?"

"I think so." Slim smiled at him. "You think this is it then? For me, I mean?"

Billy reached out and put a hand on his shoulder.

"I always knew that, for you, when it happened, that would be it."

"Ah, really? You always knew, did you?" Slim laughed.

"Yeah, honestly. It would only take one girl to hit the mark and Collette has done that." Billy turned and led Slim up the beach toward the others, who were now play-fighting and rolling in the sand. Slim put his hand on Billy's shoulder and they paused.

"Thanks mate." He smiled at Billy before grinning. "Be your turn next!" He laughed and ran up the beach away from the punch aimed at his shoulder.

"Cheeky sod." Laughed Billy.

Chapter Thirty
A Big Day Out

Maureen and Barbara were standing outside the working man's club, staring up at the poster that was pasted to the wall and saw Mickey McDonald's name on the listings.

"There he his." Said Barbara. "Told you he'd be on all week."

"Right," replied Maureen, "that's it then. We'll wait until he arrives and have a word with him."

Barbara looked at her watch and then at Maureen.

"Slight problem. It's only ten o'clock in the morning and the club doesn't open until six." She looked around and watched the bustle of the town go past, very conscious that they were two middle-aged women, staring at a drinking hole, eight hours before it opened.

"That's not important," Maureen was determined, "we know he's still here, that's the main thing. We'll come back for six and face him."

"So, what do we do for eight hours?" Barbara asked. "We can't go back to the digs, Sid and Roger have buggered off without a by-your-leave, Christ alone knows where they are and…"

"Shh!" Maureen snapped. "I'm thinking."

Barbara let her mull it over while she lit a fag, blowing smoke in the air in impatience.

Over the road, a bus pulled up and deposited passengers on the street. Maureen watched as the driver stood to wind the handle of the destination notice. It rolled around and around, names of small east coast villages flashing before her eyes until it stopped. Flamborough.

"We're going to Flamborough." She declared and looked both ways before stepping out onto the road towards the bus. Barbara looked at her stunned.

"Flamborough?" She called towards Maureen's retreating back. She realised she was being left and then shuffled off after her. "What the bloody hell are we going to do in Flamborough?"

Some miles away, off the coast, Roger and Sid were trying to balance on a fishing boat as it hit wave after wave, the sea being much rougher away from the coast.

"I feel sick." Sid tried to focus on the horizon but the occasional spray of salt water soaking him made him look away, causing his stomach to lurch.

"Shut up." Roger dismissed him. "This is lovely!" He breathed deeply, feeling the sea air doing him good after so much drink over the last few days.

The boat was old and smelt of rotting fish, not helped by the bucket of bait that was slopping around nearby, occasionally dropping pieces of fish gut coated in slime onto the deck. Sid moved his feet nearer the edge and tried not to look.

There were several other men on board. Sick of the beach, they too had escaped wives and kids by taking a day ticket out on the water, not bothered if the fish would be biting. Some had brought bottles of beer to drink while enjoying the sunshine and fresh air, which the skipper had tied in netting and thrown over the side to keep cool in the water. It dragged behind them gathering seaweed as it went while the men gathered to listen to the skipper. Sid stood at the back, near the edge, just in case.

The skipper stood on a storage box and cleared his throat to get their attention.

A small, stocky man dressed in oilskins and a thick roll-neck sweater, sleeves rolled up in deference to the heat of the sun, his face was like leather from years out on the sea. His piercing blue eyes looked out of a dark brown face which was coated in stubble as he looked at the men in turn, almost sizing them up for work.

He looked older than he probably was, standing slightly hunched but the muscles in his hands and forearms were like knotted ropes from years of physical labour, revealing a younger man. A limp rolled-up cigarette dangled from his lips, which didn't look alight but, when he sucked it, smoke billowed from his face, shielding him momentarily. All of the men stopped talking immediately at the sight of him.

"Now, we'll be another hour and then we'll anchor at t'edge of Dogger and put t'lines in." His voice was like gravel, the distinct twang of the East Yorkshire accent coming through. "There's life jackets here if you're worried 'bout 'owt." He pointed to a pile of thick orange material that could once have been serviceable life jackets, now half-rotted with mould. He made it sound like only girls wore them, so not a man moved. "So, we'll get baited up and get going."

Sid pulled urgently on Roger's shoulder as the skipper stood down and made his way to the cabin.

"I want a life jacket!" He hissed.

"Don't you dare. You'll frigging embarrass the both of us." Roger shook Sid's hand off his shoulder, smiled and nodded at the other blokes as they took up rods and took turns in the bait bucket, spearing pieces of stinking fish onto hooks.

Roger took a rod and passed one to Sid before leaning into the bucket himself. He grabbed a piece of fish and held it out to Sid, his hand oozing from something.

"Here you go." He said.

Sid went bright green and promptly threw up over the side. A cheer went up from the other blokes at the sight of Sid retching over the side. First one to go was a relief to them all, as it wouldn't look so bad if they were ill now.

"Bloody big girls blouse, you are." Muttered Roger, who leaned over and baited his friend's hook for him.

A couple of hours later they were watching their lines moving in the water, the boat rocking gently side to side, the waves settled slightly by the large sandbanks beneath them. A few fish were laid in a trough behind them, some dabs and a few herring had stopped thrashing around and were prostrate in the bottom. There were other boats out on the water, mainly trawlers going after the big cod that lived on the bank and Roger watched them lazily and wondered what Maureen was doing, He checked his watch and realised it was lunch time.

Maureen stood at the top of the slipway in Flamborough and looked down at the limestone cliffs that jutted out into the sea. The small bay beneath was azure blue and looked like a brochure advert for some faraway shore. The breeze that came off the sea was warm but strong enough to move her hair as she absent-mindedly pushed it from her eyes. There were families playing in the shallow water below, mothers and grandparents sitting in deck chairs and on rocks, fanning themselves from the heat.

She cast her mind back, it seemed like yesterday that she was here with Roger and the boys, when they'd stayed in Roger's Uncle's caravan up on the cliff top.

It must have been fifteen years ago, she thought. James was only just waddling around and Michael a robust toddler, into everything. She smiled at the memory. All those years of cheap holidays when they'd just been starting out together, borrowed caravans and tents, loaned clapped-out cars, just so they could have a holiday together.

She wondered where Roger was.

An ice cream cornet was suddenly shoved in her line of vision, her thoughts broken. Barbara was holding it out whilst she furiously licked her own cornet, trying to catch the drips from the rapidly melting ice cream.

"Here y'are." Barbara said through a mouthful. "Got you one." She shook her hand to rid herself of any drops and looked out at the bay herself. "Beautiful, isn't it?"

"Yeah." Replied Maureen, licking the cornet. "Thanks for this."

"S'alright." Barbara looked down the slip way. "Bloody steep that, isn't it? How'd they get their boats down there?" She pointed to the boats lined up on the grass behind her.

"They use a tractor and a winch." Maureen replied, not really wanting to be drawn into conversation but left with her thoughts.

"Hm." Barbara murmured her assent, looking around. "Not much else here, is there? No rides or arcades. Only one pub." She sounded disappointed.

Maureen smiled.

"No, nothing like that. Perfect for families though."

"I suppose." She took another bite of her ice cream. "Didn't you and Rog come here years ago? With the boys?"

"We did, yes, years ago, when the boys were still little. We stayed at his Uncle's caravan." She smiled again at the memory. "Tiny bloody thing. Rocked all over when the wind blew. Nearly gave Roger a nervous breakdown with two noisy kids."

"I'll bet."

They lapsed into companionable silence until it was broken by Barbara.

"So, what do we do for the next five hours?"

Maureen looked at her in exasperation.

"Just enjoy the scenery, Babs. It's beautiful. You don't need bright lights and noise to enjoy your holiday."

Barbara looked unconvinced.

Suddenly, their attention was drawn to a commotion down in the bay. A small fishing boat had pulled into the shallows and beached itself, before a man jumped down and started shouting out.

"Puffin tours! Come see the puffins. Only two-bob. First come, first served." He called out across the crescent of sand that ringed the bay and a few kids ran up to see what it was about, followed by some parents.

"Hey, shall we go?" Barbara had finished her ice cream and was wiping her mouth with a hanky.

Maureen looked amazed.

"You? On a boat?"

"Why not? It'll be nice out on the water. A bit of fresh air." She looked at Maureen who had an incredulous look on her face. "Well, it's something to do isn't it? I've always wanted to see a puffin. What else is there? Bloody pub's not even open yet." She started to walk down the slip way gingerly, her high heels catching on the ridges of the concrete. "Come on!"

Sid was starting to feel better with the sun on his face, he closed his eyes, knowing he'd hear the reel if he caught anything. They'd been out for a while now, the trough behind getting steadily full of small fish. He was secretly hoping to catch something big, to wipe the smile off the faces of the others who'd laughed at him being sick.

Roger was next to him, leaning on the side, smoking a cigarette, looking thoughtful. Sid knew better than to interrupt his thoughts but he couldn't help worrying about what was to come.

What if Mickey confirms he and Maureen had done the deed that night? What did that prove? It would end up messy; that he knew.

He heard heavy footsteps behind him so he opened his eyes and looked up. Behind them stood the skipper who had his eyes screwed up against the sun, almost making them disappear into his leather bag of a face.

"You lads having a good time?" He growled; it was almost an accusation.

"Yes, yes, we are. Thank you skip." Sid sat up straight, gabbling.

"Grand. That's grand." He looked over to Roger who was still staring out to sea. "You watching the banks, lad?" He asked.

"Yeah, I was just watching those big trawlers over there. Is it cod they're after?" Roger pointed out towards the boats that ran parallel to each other, backwards and forwards.

"Aye," Skipper stood beside him. "Big cod out there."

"Can we go and get cod?" Sid sat up and stared out to sea too. It didn't seem that far to him. The skipper laughed.

"No lad, them's Norwegian boats. They have the rights; not us." He smiled benignly at Sid. "But it'll all end up in our fish shops, no fear."

Sid looked disappointed.

"I was hoping for a big fish. You know, something to tell the wife about?"

"Well, we can move around the edge a bit further and see what there is." The skipper pointed to his right. "Out near the wrecks."

"Wrecks?" Both Roger and Sid said at once, they're interest peaked.

The skipper reached into his pocket and took out cigarette papers, a pouch of tobacco and nonchalantly rolled a cigarette, knowing he had their full attention.

"Aye, wrecks." He struck a match on the side of the boat and lit his roll-up, puffed a few times and stood straight.

"These waters are full o'wrecks. Many a man has gone to his death in these waters." He crossed himself in respect for the lost.

"What, during the war?" Asked Roger.

"Oh, long before that, lad. Hundreds of years these waters 'ave 'ad ships on 'em. Lots of 'em below, too"

Sid looked over to where the life jackets lay and wondered how quickly he could grab them. Skipper continued.

"A German submarine went down in '66. Peacetime, like. You might remember it? Nineteen lads died that night. We pulled out the only survivor. Poor bastard." He leant to look over into the water.

"Did you?" Roger's eyes were wide.

"Aye, blowing a gale it was. Nearly lost her." He looked down, reminiscing.

"Lost who?" Asked Sid.

Skipper looked at him with a glare that made Sid uncomfortable.

"This boat, that's who." He stared back out to sea. "She made it though. Badly damaged, but we made it." He patted the wood fondly, sighed and stood straight again. "I'll lift the anchor and we'll move a bit nearer." He walked slowly away before stopping and speaking again. "Sometimes, when the wind blows, it's almost like you can hear them calling out. Like they can still be saved." He walked on, shaking his head and muttering to himself.

On que, a breeze suddenly came across the water and ruffled their hair, sending a chill through them.

Roger shivered.

"God, it's like someone just walked over my grave."

"Don't say that!" Cried Sid.

Chapter Thirty-one
Growing Up

Billy had cheered up and, with afternoon wearing on, they were all getting a bit bored of laying in the sun or kicking a ball around. They'd had some company for an hour, by the way of a groups of girls who'd wandered over from the main beach areas, away from their families. But then their Dad's had come over after a while to find them and ushered them back.

Nutty flopped onto the sand next to Slim after having been in the water and thoughtfully shook his head like a dog, wetting the book he was trying to read.

"What y'reading?" He asked, picking up a towel and drying himself, grimacing as the sand on it hurt his skin.

"A book." Slim replied, non-committedly.

"Oh good." Nutty had lost interest already. "Are you seeing that bird tonight?"

"She's not a 'bird', her name is Collette." He carried on trying to read, not wanting to be drawn into conversation.

"Collette, that's it. I forgot." He paused. "So, you seeing her then?"

"Yeah, meeting her later." He abandoned the book, folding the corner of his page and wondering why he'd bothered to bring it.

"No, I mean *seeing* her. You two an item?" He emphasised the word as if Slim were stupid.

"I don't know, it's early days." He looked out at the sea shore and smiled. "I really like her though. I'd like to keep on *seeing* her." He grinned at Nutty, who got the point and lifted himself off the sand, shaking his towel out all over Slim, who flapped his arms and coughed.

"Well, it's your funeral." He said and walked over to the tent where the others were.

Or wedding, thought Slim. No, no, don't get ahead of yourself, you've only just met her.

He thought back to when he asked his mum about her meeting his dad. 'I just knew' she'd said.

Well, he knew.

Knew that this was it. He smiled again. Then he frowned. What if she didn't feel the same? Oh shit.

Billy called out to him and he lifted himself up, dusted himself down and, picking up his book, trotted over to where the others were.

"We were just having a discussion about tonight, Slim." Billy said, squinting as the afternoon sun got a bit lower in a cloudless sky, bathing everything in a warm, golden light.

"And?" He asked.

"Well, Me and James want to try that disco over on the south shore as we saw loads of women going in" Said Michael, "and we didn't get there last night as this one," he gestured towards Billy, "had a sulk on."

"I don't have a sulk on!" Billy threw sand at him.

"And I was just saying I wasn't bothered what we did as long as it involved beer." Nutty chipped in.

"So, it comes down to you and Billy." James said with finality.

"Ah, I'm not fussed. I'll do whatever." Billy flopped back on the sand, his arm over his eyes. All eyes turned to Slim.

"You're asking me? You've never asked me what I wanted." Slim said. "I've just always followed you lot." He walked over to the tent and, lifting the flap, threw his book onto his sleeping bag. The others continued looking at him.

"So, you're happy for us to go to the disco?" Asked James.

"Do what you like. I'm off to meet Collette." He replied. He reached into the tent again and brought out his wash bag. "I'm off to get ready." He walked off down the sand, towards the water, leaving them in a stunned silence. Billy just smiled into the crook of his arm.

The three of them watched him gingerly wade into the sea, before ducking himself under and rubbing his head and body with soap.

"Do you know," Said James, "in all the time I've known him, I've never heard him say anything like that."

"No, nor me." Nutty said.

Billy's muffled voice came from behind them.

"Well, people change you know." He took his arm off his face, stood up slowly and looked out to where Slim was splashing around in the water, surrounded by a ring of soap suds. "He's grown up these past few days." He looked at the three of them, who were staring at him, confused looks on their faces. "It wouldn't do you lot any harm either." Billy reached for his own wash kit and followed Slim down to the water, leaving them thinking it over.

"I think I'm offended." Said Michael.

"Me too." Nutty pushed the sand away from him with his long legs and leaned back. They paused while they watched Billy and Slim laughing and chatting in the water.

"So, are we going to the disco or not?" Asked James.

Chapter Thirty-Two
Facing the Music

Barbara was still green from the boat ride.

They were sitting on the veranda of the pub, waiting for the bus to take them back to Bridlington and to the face-to-face with Mickey McDonald.

Maureen didn't feel too good herself.

Barbara tried to take a sip of the half of lager that was sitting in front of her but the smell made her feel worse, so she put it down again.

"Urgh." Was all she could say, trying to stifle a belch of bile.

"I told you, you wouldn't like it." Maureen said, sipping her own drink.

"Who knew little birds like that crapped so much?" Barbara replied.

They'd been on the boat for an hour, all was going fine, with Barbara excited at seeing the little colourful puffins bobbing in the water and up on the limestone cliffs, until the acrid smell of generations of guano had hit her.

The sides of the cliffs were covered, blending in with the white of the limestone cliffs. The combination of that and the bobbing of the little boat in the water had turned her stomach to the point she thought she was going to die. Then she wished that she would.

As they were sitting there, lost in their own thoughts, one of trepidation; one of sickness, the bus arrived with a grind of gears, the exhaust fumes blowing across the road and straight onto the veranda. Barbara's chair was thrown back as, taking in a mouthful of fumes, she clapped her hand to her mouth and made a dash for the ladies.

Maureen sighed, stood, and then walked over to the bus driver.

"Two for Bridlington here, love." She fished the return ticket from her bag and gave it to the driver. "Can you give her a minute?" She nodded towards the pub. "She's in the ladies."

Sid stepped off the boat onto the harbour side and felt like kissing the ground. He'd survived.

Roger stepped off behind him and put his on his shoulder. "Well done, mate."

"Never, ever, again." Was all he could say, still feeling like his legs were jelly from the motion of the boat, his stomach going up and down.

The sun was getting lower now and Roger checked his watch as the trawler roared back into life, having deposited it passengers, it moved off to a mooring further in the harbour.

"Come on, it's just gone six. We'd best make our way to the club." He strode on with a confidence that belied his nervousness. Sid took a deep breath and trotted after him.

Maureen and Barbara stepped off the bus, the journey having done nothing for Barbara's constitution, and both looked at the club on the opposite side of the road.

Maureen checked her watch; it was six o'clock and the door was now open. She took a deep breath, steeled herself and moved to step inside.

Barbara put a hand on her shoulder, halting her.

"Are you sure about this, 'Reen?" She asked, her face worried at what might be about to happen.

Maureen paused.

"Yes. I have to know. I don't want any doubt in Roger's mind. Or mine." She carried on walking.

Once inside the club, the sudden gloom made them blink, even with the concert hall lights on full, the sunlight outside had caused them to go blind for just one minute. They let their eyes get used to the change and then saw the Steward as he placed beer mats and ashtrays on each table, polishing them over with a bar towel first. He looked up when he heard their footsteps on the parquet floor.

"Hello ladies. Early start is it?" He grinned at them. "What'll it be?"

"Half a lager, ple…" Barbara started but was interrupted by Maureen.

"Can you let Mickey know that there's someone here to talk to him?" She said in a voice filled with determination.

"The turn? What do you want to see him for?" He asked, pausing mid-beer mat. "Fans are you?"

"Could you just tell him please? Tell him Maureen is here to see him. Maureen from York. He'll know who I am." She clasped her arms in front of her and stared the man down.

"Alright, alright. I'll tell him." He put down his towel and walked to a door at the side of the stage. "Bloody lucky he's still here, anyway. After that fight the other night. Bloody jealous husbands. Bad for business." He carried on muttering as he pushed open the door and walked through.

"I'm not sure about this, 'Reen." Whispered Barbara.

"What are you whispering for? There's no bugger here!" Maureen's body language was tense but she would see this through. She had to.

They heard voices from behind the stage and they could make out the Geordie accent of Mickey as it got closer to the door.

"Alreet, alreet, I'm going." Mickey stepped through the door, still looking behind him, followed by the Steward who merely pointed at Maureen and Barbara.

"There. Two lasses to see you." The Steward walked away and made off the bar area to set it up but also to get a good vantage point of Mickey's visitors.

Mickey looked over, allowing his eyes to get accustomed to the light then realised who it was.

"Maureen?"

"Hello Mickey." Maureen called as he walked across the dance floor towards her.

"What are you doing here?" He asked. He held his hands out as if to take hers but she kept them firmly clenched.

"Hello Mickey!" Piped up Barbara.

Mickey merely glanced at her and nodded before turning back to Maureen. He suddenly looked uncomfortable.

"It's good to see you but if it's about the other night, I'm sorry." His face was suddenly apologetic after the initial happiness at seeing her.

"No, no, it's not about the other night…" She started to say then suddenly, she was lost for words.

Barbara looked between the two of them, the gap of silence making everything uncomfortable. She wished she were anywhere else right now, but here. Well, if 'Reen wasn't going to say anything; she would.

"It's about that night twenty years ago!" She called, a little shrilly, her nerves getting the better of her.

"Babs!" Maureen hissed.

"Twenty years ago? I don't understand. What about it?" Asked Mickey, still looking confused.

Maureen coughed as Barbara opened her mouth to say something else but Maureen merely silenced her with a look and she shut her mouth. She turned back to look at Mickey. "Did we, erm…what I mean to say is, did you…"

She got no further as, behind them, the door swung shut and standing there were Roger and Sid.

"Maureen?" Roger could feel the anger rising in him.

"Barbara?" Asked Sid in a voice that was more like a call for help than a question.

"Roger!" Maureen spun around to face her husband, the fear forming a knot in her stomach.

"What the bloody hell are you doing here?" Roger asked, starting to walk towards them.

"I could ask you the same thing!" She retorted.

Roger's mind was doing somersaults. Why was she here? Was she going to leave him for Mickey? He balled his fists ready.

"Ey, ey, we'll have no trouble here!" The Steward shouted across the bar, wishing he had some back-up, fearing the worst. He'd only just finished cleaning the place, he thought.

"I've come to see him!" Said Roger, pointing at Mickey, teeth clenched, the aggression in his body clear for everyone to see. Sid grabbed his arm.

"Roger, you said there's be no trouble." With one arm on Roger, he reached out to Barbara and pulled her over with the other towards him, afraid of a fight breaking out.

"There'll be no trouble, Sid." Maureen snapped. "Just calm down." She stepped towards Roger. "Why are you here?" She pleaded.

"I need to know the truth, 'Reen. I need to know." He was still tense but had started to relax a little.

Looking at Maureen he softened, sorry that she was witness to this.

Maureen took his hand in hers and unclenched the fist.

"That's why I'm here too." She said quietly.

"You what?" Roger asked.

"You what?" Echoed Sid. Barbara took his hand and nodded at him.

"After what you said last night, when you said it didn't matter, I knew it did really." She felt the tears springing up in her eyes. "I didn't realise you'd been carrying this for twenty years."

Roger looked down at the floor.

"Why haven't you said anything?" She asked.

"I don't think I really wanted to know but, after the other night." He paused and looked into her eyes. "I think I do."

"Yeah, me too. We both need to know." She smiled at him. "For our own peace of mind."

"Excuse me." Mickey spoke up, startling the others who had all but forgotten he was there. "But what is it you need to know? And what is it to do with me?"

Roger's heckles went straight up and he took a step forward towards Mickey. Maureen blocked his way. She turned to Mickey.

"Mickey, that night we went out in York, after the fight you and Roger had."

"Which he started." Mickey jumped in.

"You were chatting up my fiancée!" Cried Roger in defence.

"She wasn't your fiancée that night, pal." Mickey squared his shoulders and Roger responded, eager to get to him.

"Stop it the pair of you!" Maureen shouted.

She was between them both, arms outstretched, one hand on each of their chests.

"Christ, you're like a couple of kids!" She felt them both relax slightly so she let her hands drop. "Mickey, you have to tell me, because I have no memory of anything. What happened that night?"

Mickey looked at her, then at the others. He was stunned. "What happened? After twenty years, you're asking me what happened?"

"Yes!" All of them shouted, including the Steward who was captivated by what was going on.

Mickey sighed and pulled out a chair, gesturing to the others to sit too. Maureen and Barbara sat and Sid pulled out a chair but saw that Roger had no intention, so he quietly pushed it back and stood next to him in a show of solidarity.

"Look, it was a long time ago…" He started talking.

"Just tell us." Roger interrupted, fearing the worst.

"Let him speak, Roger!" Maureen hissed.

Mickey leaned forward and rested his hands on his knees before looking at each of them in turn.

"That night, after we had a scrap in the street, I felt awful. I hate fighting; hate it. It was embarrassing."

He looked at Roger. "I honestly didn't know the situation between you two. I saw Maureen in the bar and recognised her from the factory so, asked her for a drink." He saw Roger looking at Maureen so he continued. "There was nothing in it, honestly, just a friendly drink." He watched as they all raised their eyebrows at him, disbelieving. "Alright, so, I fancied her. Who wouldn't?"

Roger tensed as Mickey spoke.

"But, if I'd known you two were an item, I wouldn't have done that." He sat back, his arms out, palms up in a conciliatory way.

"So, you had a drink and then I came in…" Roger wanted to move him on.

"Pissed. You came in pissed." Stated Maureen.

"Alright!" Roger gestured for Mickey to continue.

"So, it ended up on the street. You'd had a skin full and you weren't nice to her. I wanted to defend her." He paused. "Stupid to fight though." He added.

Roger looked at his feet, shame-faced.

"Sorry." He muttered.

"You should be. You were a complete bastard." Barbara piped up before Sid looked at her sternly. "And you weren't much better!" She sniffed at him.

Sid couldn't answer that.

"Anyway, after what happened, I walked off. Didn't think the club would want me back in there, not after a punch-up with one of their members, so I walked into town to cool off."

"Did you not get paid?" Sid asked before being shushed by the others.

Mickey smiled sadly.

"No, I didn't get paid. And the factory gave me my cards the next day too. They'd heard all about it." He stood from the chair and walked around it; resting his hands on the back.

"So, what happened then?" Asked Roger.

"I followed you, didn't I?" Maureen spoke. Her head tilted at Roger. "I wanted to apologise for your behaviour."

"Aye, you did." Mickey said. "You showed me around York and we had a few drinks. It was nice. I'd never been before." His face darkened. "Never been back, neither."

There was a heavy silence as they watched Mickey move back around the chair before sitting down again, heavily.

He picked up a beer mat and started turning it over in his hands, the memories coming back. Was that really twenty years ago?

Maureen took the initiative.

"But after that Mickey, the bit I don't remember."

Mickey looked up again and shrugged.

"You'd had a few before we went out. I think it was too much. So, I walked you back to your digs. You were unsteady on your feet, so I thought I'd better." He looked at Roger who had an incredulous look on his face, mirrored by Sid and Barbara's.

"So, you just dropped her off at her place?" Roger asked, his voice low, willing Mickey to lie, to drop himself in it.

"No, I took her in, made sure she was alright." Mickey's voice was still innocent.

"And that's it?" Roger asked.

"That's it." Mickey sat back. "That's all there was to it."

Maureen was watching him, knowing that it wasn't as clear cut as that. The note and the flower. He'd left those. He'd been in her room.

Roger was thinking the same thing.

"Mickey," Maureen leaned forward, she knew that Roger knew more so she decided to bite the bullet. "You were in my room though."

"Yeah, I found your carnation on the bedroom floor the next day." Roger's voice was like flint now, staring hard at Mickey.

So that's how he knew, thought Maureen. He'd found it.

"So, what really happened?" Roger continued.

Mickey's face dropped realising he'd been caught out then his look turned to one of resignation.

"When we got to your bedroom door," He spoke to Maureen directly, "you practically fell through it. So, I put you on the bed and tucked you in."

Roger snorted like a bull.

"I waited with you a little while, to make sure you weren't going to be ill and that's when I wrote that note"

"What note?" Asked Roger, amazed.

"I wrote a note saying thank you for the evening and wishing her all the best." Mickey's voice was still innocent.

"Thank you for the evening?" Roger snarled. "What else were you thanking her for?"

"Roger!" Snapped Maureen.

"Well, you can't tell me that, a red-bloodied male would take a young lass home, to her bedroom and not take advantage!" Roger exploded.

"No!" Cried Mickey. "That's not what happened. You have to believe me." He looked between all three of them, the look of disbelief on their faces. "I wouldn't have done anything like that!"

Maureen didn't know whether to be relieved or offended.

"Do you expect me to believe that?" Roger snarled at him.

"Yes! I wouldn't!" His face crumpled and his shoulders sagged. "I couldn't."

Silence.

"Couldn't?" Maureen ventured.

The steward was nearly falling over the bar to hear what was coming next, desperately hoping no-one else would come in for a drink.

"No. Couldn't." Mickey looked between Roger and Sid.

"You two did national service, did you?" He asked.

"Well, yes, we did." Roger was flustered now, wondering where this was going.

"Me too." Mickey said, his voice full of sadness and regret. "Where were you two?" He asked.

"What has this got to do with anything!" Shouted Roger.

"Shut up, Rog. Let him speak." Barbara snapped at him.

"Germany." Sid said. "Osnabrück."

"Ah, nice that." Mickey was talking to the floor. He looked up and took a deep breath. "Korea, me. 'Withdrawal from theatre', they called it. Bloody shambles from my perspective." He sighed. "Nineteen, I was."

Both Roger and Sid sucked air in through their teeth. They'd been lucky.

"Took some shrapnel in the…" He acknowledged there were ladies present. "Well, use your imagination."

Both Sid and Roger coughed and swallowed.

"So," he continued, "you've nothing to fear on that score. I wouldn't. I couldn't."

Silence filled the air, all of them looking both in amazement and with pity at the man in front of them.

"So, you can never have kids?" Asked Maureen, reaching out and touching him on the arm.

Mickey looked at her and smiled.

"No, not me. Safe pair of hands, me."

"Thank you." She said.

"For what?"

"For looking after me that night."

"Ah, it wasn't just me pet." He stood again and looked down at her, into her eyes. "That housemate of yours, what was her name? She took over and sorted things out. I just walked back to my own digs, like."

Maureen turned in her seat and looked at Roger.

"Satisfied? That's what happened." She said, an edge to her voice.

"Yeah, yeah." Roger muttered. He looked up at Mickey. "I'm sorry mate about, well, you know. Everything." "It's all forgotten." Mickey patted the air with his hands. "I'd best get ready." He took a few steps away from them towards the stage before looking back. "Will you stay for the entertainment?" He smiled his winning smile.

Chapter Thirty-three
Last Night at the OK Corral

James raised his pint glass in a toast, lager dripping down the sides and over his fingers.

"To Slim! May he be happy and victorious!" He drank deeply.

"Hooray!" Michael and Nutty cheered in mock salute whilst Billy just sat quietly and shook his head.

They were sitting in the pub on North Marine Drive, minus Slim, who had gone to meet Collette, having a few beers before moving off to the disco.

The pub was busy but not so full as to be raucous and they could hear themselves speak over the hum of conversation. The evening light was mellow, the sun just going down and a thin wave of sea fog was starting to cover the sands.

Billy watched seagulls as they flew low over the front, looking for scraps of food and he sighed.

He looked at the three lads he was with and, feeling fond of them, he knew his place was here, with them, at this moment in time but he couldn't let go of the overwhelming sense of time slipping away from him. As if he was missing something.

"What's up, Billy?" Nutty asked through a mouthful of crisps.

"Nothing. I'm alright."

"You'll cheer up when you get to the disco and amongst all those birds." He nudged him.

Billy forced a smile.

He knew he wouldn't.

Suddenly, the doors opened and in walked Slim holding Collette's hand. Catching his eye, Billy waved him over.

"Hello stranger!" He said before turning to Collette. "Hello love, how are you?"

"I'm ok thanks Billy." She looked around the others sat at the table and pulled on Slim's hand.

"What? Oh, yes, sorry. This is Michael, James and Nutty." He waved his hand noncommittedly at the other three sitting there. He smiled at her. "Lads, this is Collette."

"Figured that one out, Slim." Michael said, standing to shake her hand. The other two stood as well, leaning over the glasses on the table to greet her.

"Can I get you a drink, love?" Asked Nutty

"Ooh, yes please. I'll have a pint." She sat down next to Michael and smiled.

"Yeah, me too, please Nutty." Slim sat beside her, proud of her.

Nutty looked at the others and mouthed 'a pint?' before striding over to the bar.

The lads all gave her the once-over as she smiled after Nutty then looked at Slim.

Collectively, they thought she was pretty in a small, compact sort of way, her blonde hair loosely tied back with a wide mouth, revealing white teeth. Her clothes were loose and fashionable, in a street-wise kind of way, her jeans and blouse cut in such a way that they showed her voluptuous body but weren't too revealing. She seemed to be very much enamoured with Slim, which they all thought amazing.

She turned to see them all staring at her, making things a little awkward.

"So," Michael attempted to start a conversation, "Slim hasn't told us that much about you?" He noted Slim's hand on her thigh and hers on his, stroking his cords.

"Oh, there's not much to know, really." She smiled, one that made them instinctively smile back. They liked her.

"I work at Sara Lees making cakes…"

Perfect for Slim, they thought.

"And I help out mum and dad with the guest house in the season. You know, with the beds and stuff. Make breakfast sometimes."

"You're a busy lass, then?" James said, wanting desperately to be part of the conversation.

"Yes, pretty much." She laughed. "It's rare I get a summer to myself."

Billy watched her and Slim together, hopelessly happy and he smiled as Nutty arrived back at the table carrying a tray carrying six pints of lager, which he lowered with difficulty, slopping some on the table.

"Oops, sorry. Here you go." He shoved himself onto the seat next to Slim, causing everyone to shift up as he grabbled a pint and raised it. "Cheers! Nice to meet you, love."

Everyone else grabbed a glass, Slim handing one to Collette and they touched glasses.

"Cheers!"

Collette sipped her drink; the pint glass looking huge in her small hand and watched the others gulping it down.

"We're off to the disco tonight, if you two want to join us?" James spoke again as he wiped his mouth.

Slim and Collette looked at each other.

"Er, sorry lads, we can't." Slim replied, half a smile on his face.

"Oh, too good for us now, eh?" Nutty nudged him, causing is drink to spill.

"No, it's just that.."

"It's alright Slim. Don't worry about him. You two go and spend some time together." Billy said. There was a pause in the conversation before James butted in.

"What's wrong with the disco, then? You can be together in there. With us. I don't get it." He said before Billy cuffed him around the head lightly. "Ow, what was that for?"

"Shut up. They've made plans. None of which involve us." Collette laughed at them.

"Thanks for the invite, it's just we're having dinner at mum and dad's tonight." She turned back to Slim. "They'd like to meet Slim."

A hush descended over the table, Nutty, James and Michael put their glasses on the table in stunned silence and looked at each other.

"Parents? Already?" Asked Nutty.

"Wow, you don't hang about, do you?" Michael added.

Both Slim and Collette grinned and Billy smiled at them.

"Ah, good for you Slim." He said and raised his glass again. The others grudgingly smiled and did the same.

Billy watched as they all drank and noticed how the dynamic had changed, how different they all were and how the odd year or two between them, really made a difference.

They drank for another hour, chatting and laughing, the lads asking Collette about growing up in Bridlington and her asking about their life in York, the factory and all growing up together.

They waxed lyrical about Slim's exploits, leaving out the more embarrassing parts and the evening wore on.

People in the bar came and went and the lights came on as it got dark outside, some people shuffling home, others heading to different pubs as groups mingled, then dispersed.

Michael checked his watch and looked up.

"Time we was off!" He announced, draining his glass and standing, gesturing to the others to do the same.

With a sigh, Billy did the same, following the lead by the others and they all made their way outside into the warm evening, the coloured bulbs that were strung between the lampposts casting pools of light onto the pavement.

A fresh breeze was blowing off the sea, clearing the mist and there were people strolling on the sands, enjoying the evening air.

"Well," Slim said, "we'll be off. Have a good night at the disco."

"It was lovely to meet you all at last." Collette pushed her arm through Slim's, smiled at them all and they began walking towards the old town, away from the front.

The lads waved them off before turning and heading further along the front.

They fell into an amiable stroll, hands in pockets, four abreast on the pavement, none of them speaking until James broke the silence.

"She seems nice, that Collette."

"Yeah, just what Slim needs, a girl like that." Michael replied.

"Seems a bit soon though." Nutty added.

"Soon for what?" Asked Michael.

"Well, meeting the folks. Seems a bit fast." He paused. "And serious."

"It is serious." Billy said. "He's serious about her."

The others looked at him as they walked, curious about this new, reflective Billy.

"Still, just seems a bit too soon to me." Nutty sniffed.

They continued walking, the lights and music from the disco were discernible further along the street.

"Have you ever taken a bird to meet your parents, Nutty?" Asked James.

Nutty thought about the question, not knowing whether to answer it or not.

"Yeah," he said, "once I have."

"And you're still single? How's that?" Michael retorted, the rest of them breaking into laughter as they reached the door of the disco and, nodding at the bouncers on the door, they strolled in, ready for the night.

The club hummed with beat of music as the chart hits pounded across the dancefloor, the babble of shouted conversations adding to the cacophony that hit their senses as they walked down the lobby and into the club. In the darkness, they could make out crowds of people filling the wide, circular room.

The bar lined the wall to the right with men and women either leant against it drinking, or with others waving notes in the air, waiting to get served. The staff behind were busy, filling pint glasses at the same time as turning to the optics to dispense spirits, taking money and giving out change, all the while taking the next order. They were smooth with their movements, almost in time with the music.

The lads scanned the scene before them like soldiers before battle, identifying targets and their routes to them.

"Whose round is it?" Shouted Nutty, leaning into the group to be heard.

No-one replied.

"I'll go." Said Billy after a pause. He turned to the bar, rummaging in his pockets for his money. The others watched in amazement at a rare event. Billy was normally the first one onto the dancefloor to check on the talent.
As he got to the bar, the others began some tentative steps further into the gloom, the flashing lights were disorientating as they fumbled their way down the steps, slippery from spilt drinks, to find a spare table where they could plan their attack.
Billy leant over the bar with a fiver in his hands, trying to get the barman's attention. Unwittingly, he nudged another man as he did so, causing him to slop beer from his glass onto the bar.
"Sorry, mate." Billy said. "Didn't mean to knock you."
The man turned to him with a snarl on his face, his eyes half-closed from what Billy realised was a serious skin full of beer. Oh shit, he thought.
"Watch where your going, lad." The man slurred, standing to his full height, which was a few inches more than Billy. The man poked him in his chest with a hand that was like a shovel. "I've spilt me beer now."
Billy looked at his pint glass and saw only a drop had come out but that obviously didn't matter. The guy was brewing for trouble. He smiled his winning smile.
"I'll buy you another. No trouble, eh?"
"You'd better." The man growled as Billy managed to get someone's attention, just in time.
"Four lagers and, er," He looked at the man staring at him. "And another for my friend here." He tried to sound cheerful as he said it, feeling the aggression emanating towards him.

The pints landed on the bar and Billy pushed, gently, a pint of what looked like diesel fuel to the man who took it in his huge paw. He now held two pints, one in each hand. Still staring at Billy, he lifted the earlier pint, lifted it to his mouth and drained it in a few gulps, then slammed the glass back onto the bar, never once taking his eyes off Billy's. He wiped his mouth with his sleeve and leant in again, his lip curled.

"I'm watching you." He snarled, covering Billy's face in spit and beer, before standing unsteadily and staggering off.

"Who was that?" Michael was behind him now, having come to help carry the glasses.

"It doesn't matter." Billy snapped back as he watched the man take up a seat near the door, still with his eyes on Billy. "Come on. Where are the others?"

They turned and Michael led the way to a corner table that was raised high at the edge of the dancefloor, the others standing, watching the groups of women dancing around their handbags as Billy and Michael put down their drinks.

"Cheers!" Shouted Nutty and James.

All four of them began drinking, with Billy trying to calm the adrenalin that was coursing through his system. He couldn't see the man anymore; his seat was empty.

Probably gone to find another mug to get a free beer, he thought, so he put him out of his mind and began to survey the dancefloor with the others.

A few beers later and the lads were well oiled, Billy was in another corner chatting to a girl, while the other three were laughing with a group of older women who were obviously on a night out, away from their husbands.

From out of nowhere, the man from earlier appeared, stumbling through the crowds of people, pushing them aside, glasses crashing to the floor, causing everyone to look up.

"Ey, you!" He bellowed, pointing at the table where the three lads were chatting to the women.

One of the women, a tall blonde, looked up at him before a look of horror came over her.

"Oh shite!" She shouted, quickly standing and smoothing her skirt down.

The group, including the three lads, all stood at the commotion, looking between the large barrel-chested drunk before them and the women they had been speaking to.

"Who's that?" Shouted James, pointing at the man.

The blonde turned to look at him.

"Me ex-husband." She said firmly, with a slightly apologetic look on her face.

The three turned to look at each other, with 'oh fuck' looks on their faces.

The man stumbled to the table and roughly took his wife by the arm, as she struggled to free herself. He pushed his face into hers.

"Get yerself home." He turned to the lads. "I'll sort these out."

The women snapped her arm free.

"I'll go home when I bloody well like. You don't tell me what to do anymore." She shouted back at him.

The record that had been playing suddenly scratched to a halt and the lights came on, causing everyone to groan and squint suddenly. All eyes from the dance floor turned towards the scene as the crowd halted, mid dance-pose.

The lads began edging themselves away from the scene from behind the table with Michael furiously gesturing to Billy to get with them. Billy saw what was happening and realised who was causing all the trouble. Jesus, he thought, this looked bad.

He tiptoed away from the girl he was talking with and moved to the other side of the dance floor, hoping the man from earlier wouldn't see him, as he waved back at Michael and pointed at the door.

"Let's go." He mouthed at them.

Michael nodded and pulled the other two away towards where Billy was standing.

Despite the man and woman arguing, the drunk noticed them moving and as he turned his head, he caught sight of Billy gesturing to them.

"And where do you think you're going?" He shouted at them.

All four of them froze to the spot.

On the steps leading up from the dancefloor toward the exit, three other men had suddenly appeared and they were staring at the scene before them. All of them were big, dressed similarly, with tight t-shirts revealing bulging muscles.

Oh good, thought Billy, the bouncers have arrived.

"What's up, Geoff?" One of them called over to the drunk who was still trying to manhandle his ex-wife out of the club. He turned to look at the man who'd called his name and smiled with evil satisfaction. He gestured to the four lads trying to make their escape.

"Those four there." He took a step towards them. "They were chatting up our wives." He suddenly sounded very sober and alert as he spoke.

Billy's face collapsed in a groan. They weren't the bouncers; just the drunk's mates.

Around them, a pin could have been heard dropping as the crowd of dancers began melting away, backing themselves into corners.

One of the big men on the steps took a slow step down toward them, his muscles tensed as he focussed on Billy.

"Is that right? Were you chatting them up?" He growled at him.

"What? No! I…" He looked to the others for support only to see three pairs of eyes looking very afraid.

He slumped his shoulders and looked at the man wearily. "Look, we're just having a good time on holiday. No harm done, eh?"

The man stepped down to the same level as Billy but regardless, Billy still had to look up at him.

"No harm?" He turned to look at his companions up on the top step, who were smirking. "No harm, he says." He took a step closer to Billy, so close, Billy could see the broken blood vessels in his nose. He lifted his massive hands in front of Billy's face and flexed them, the skin like leather but cracked at the joints, like an old jacket that had been worn for years.

"You see these, do ya?" He snarled down at Billy.

Billy swallowed. Hard.

"Yes. Yes, I do."

"These have been pulling rope for weeks out at sea."

Oh shit, a pissed-up fisherman, thought Billy.

"And all I've wanted to do with them is to hold nice things, like pints of beer…" He rubbed one of the hands across his chin, sounding like sandpaper on wood. "…and soft things, like my wife." He nodded towards the women over at the table who looked anxious at the scene.

"But do you know the softest thing a man like me can do with these?" He raised his hand again.

I can guess, thought Billy, but said nothing.

"Is to give you lads a good slap." He turned his hand so the back of it was close to Billy's face, where he could see what were, unmistakably, prison tattoos.

Billy took his eyes off the hand and looked the big fisherman in the eyes.

For some, inexplicable reason, he really didn't care what this bloke in front of him would do. The last two days had seen him reflect on his life, where it was going and that night, in that place, watching Slim walk into the sunset with a girl, in love, had brought all of his frustrations to bear.

He felt like a fight. He just didn't care anymore.

He moved closer to the big man until their noses were almost touching, seeing his own reflection in the glassiness of his eyes and he said something he knew he would remember for the rest of his life.

If he lived past tonight.

"Softer still…" Billy dropped his voice an octave, "…is if you give me a wank."

He heard the sharp intake of breath all around him but never took his eyes off the other man's.

The silence seemed to last for an age as the big fisherman let Billy's words sink into his drink-addled brain.

He raised his eyebrows and then smiled, revealing broken teeth.

Billy smiled back.

Then the world exploded.

Two hours later, Nutty, sitting on a kerb stone, dabbing his split lip with a handkerchief, raised a painful arm to check his watch. The glass was shattered but he could make out the time, amazed it was still working after the battering it had taken. Next to him, James was leaning forward pinching his nose, making sure the bleeding had stopped and Michael was standing, his head against the wall, wishing his headache would disappear.

"It's ten past two." Nutty mumbled through his swollen mouth.

"And we're still here." Michael groaned, the effort of talking hurting him even more.

Behind them were the bright lights of the police station, where Billy was helping them with their enquiries.

"How much longer?" Nutty asked, dribbling slightly.

No-one answered him as it was the same question he'd been asking for over an hour.

Suddenly, the doors opened and out stepped Billy. His shirt was torn and a black eye was starting to appear but he was smiling. Behind him followed a police sergeant, who walked him over to where the others were.

"Right, off you go." He spoke to Billy but looked at the others who struggled to raise themselves. "And remember what I've said."

"Yes, thank you officer." Billy replied to the retreating back of the policeman.

The others gathered around him.

"What did they say?" James asked urgently.

"What happened to the fisherman?" Nutty joined in, not letting Billy have time to answer the first question.

Michael just held his aching head.

Billy lifted his hands to hush them.

"Let's just say we're not the first holiday-makers to be picked on by these lads." He smiled at his friends, though it hurt his face to do so.

"What do you mean?" Michael finally roused himself.

"They make a habit of it. Loaded with money, full of drink, they start a fight with anyone." He gestured with is head back to the police station. "They're old mates in there, them lot. They have them locked up every time they're back in harbour."

"And it was our turn tonight?" Nutty asked.

"Yeah." Replied Billy.

"So, you're in the clear? You know, for the fight?" James looked at him, wide-eyed. .

Billy looked at the stars above and breathed deeply after the fetid air of a police cell, before looking back at them.

"On one condition." He said, tugging at the ripped fabric of his shirt.

"Which is?"

"We have to leave town." Billy ushered them down the pavement, away from the station, eager to leave it behind. As they walked, Michael took hold of his shoulder, causing Billy to wince.

"What do you mean, 'we have to leave town'? This wasn't our fault!"

"No," replied Billy, "they know that. But these blokes have friends." He turned to look at the other three. "Do you want to spend another week looking over your shoulder?" He carried on walking, leaving the other three behind him in stunned silence until he turned to look at them.

"And we're breaking several bye-laws for camping on the beach." He paused. "We're going home."

He delivered the final statement and began walking,
smiling to himself.
Good riddance, he thought.

Chapter Thirty-four
And the winner is...

Maureen was tapping her feet under the table with her fingers matching the rhythm of the music on the side of her glass.

The club was heaving with people, many of them recognisable from the factory and there'd been smiles and waves of greeting all around as the night got into full swing. Next to her sat Roger, who was laughing loudly along with the next table, cigarettes being passed around and the tables full of glasses.

On the stage was Mickey McDonald, singing tunes from the fifties, smiling and winking at the couples in front of him, dancing away, politely colliding with each other.

Amongst them were Sid and Barbara, twirling with abandon, Barbara throwing her head back and laughing every time Sid made a show of breaking off into full swing mode, crouching and twisting, his ankles and knees attempting to move in different directions at the same time. Maureen felt Roger's hand find hers as he gripped it tightly and she turned to smile at him.

"Alright?" He asked above the noise of the club.

Maureen just nodded at him, smiling.

On the stage, Mickey finished his number and the couples on the dancefloor broke apart, turned and applauded.

"Thank you, thank you." He called. He pointed to the dancefloor. "And, I have to say, there some terrific movers in here tonight!"

Applause and cheers sounded.

"Now, I have to dedicate this next number to some people here on holiday from York!"

The place erupted with cheers and whistles as he stepped to the front of the stage. "Where are you? Maureen and Roger?" He wafted at the cigarette smoke with his arm, trying to see beyond the bright stage lights.

Out of the gloom, he saw Roger stand up, waving and pointing enthusiastically at Maureen as he tried to pull her up too. She stood reluctantly, slapping Roger's arm affectionately. She could see Sid and Barbara smiling and clapping their hands at them.

"Ah, there you are, you two." He paused and turned to the two guys sitting behind him on keyboard and drums, said a few words away from the microphone and, as they cued up an introduction, Mickey turned back to the audience and continued talking.

"I just want to say, it's been a pleasure meeting you both again, after all these years and I want to wish you well for the future."

He stepped back and turned to the musicians to cue them in as the audience applauded.

Maureen leant into Roger.

"What's he doing?" She hissed.

He shrugged his shoulders at her but was still smiling as Mickey began to sing.

"*They, asked me how I knew…..my true love was true….*"

Maureen's mouth fell open. Her favourite song. Ever. She turned to Roger.

"*I of course replied… something, deep inside… cannot be denied…*"

"You told him?" She asked, wide-eyed.

Roger nodded.

"*They, said someday you'll find… all who love are blind…*"

He took her hand and kissed it.

"Would you like to dance?" He asked.

She was stunned. He never danced, ever.

She just nodded as he took her hand and led her to the dancefloor. The crowd parted to let them on and they held each other tightly, swaying with the music.

Around them, the other couples did the same, the soft lilting tones of Mickey's voice carrying them off, back twenty years, to their youth.

"When your heart's on fire… you must realise… smoke gets in your eyes…"

Maureen's head was on Roger's shoulder as she whispered into his ear.

"When did you tell him, this was my favourite song?"

"Ah, I left a note behind the bar when I went to get some drinks." He moved his head so he could see into her eyes. "I wanted you to know I always remember important things."

She frowned slightly.

"I think I've learnt that on this holiday!"

Roger laughed and put his head next to hers.

"Besides," He spoke directly into her ear. "He didn't know any Pat Boone numbers."

She cuffed around the head lightly while he chuckled in her ear.

A few hours later, the four of them were saying their goodbyes at the club door, shaking hands and calling out to friends when a voice behind them made them both jump.

"Well, I'm glad you've had a good evening." Mickey spoke. He was wearing casual clothes with a suit carrier slung over one shoulder and a bag over the other.

"Ah, Mickey!" Called Roger. "Thanks for that fella, we've had a great evening."

Maureen did a double take at her husband, greeting the man who he'd accused of fathering his first-born child like an old friend.

"Ah, no bother," said Mickey. "I'm just glad we could leave things like this. Y'know. Friendly, like." His soft Geordie accent was more pronounced off-stage but his smile remained the same.

Sid reached over to shake his hand and Barbara leant over to give him a peck on the cheek.

"We had a great night, Mickey," she said, "and I'm sorry for all of the, er, well, you know. Earlier."

"Ah, no, forget it." Mickey shifted awkwardly. "Well, have to be getting off now."

"Where are you going?" Maureen asked.

"I've got to drive up to Scarborough tonight. My next gig is there." He smiled at her, just a little sadly.

"So, we won't see you again?" Roger asked but was quickly punched on the arm by Maureen. "No, I just meant we were just getting to know each other, you know…"

"I know what you meant, it's ok." Mickey shifted the weight of his bag on his shoulder. "No, I won't see you again. After Scarborough, I'm off for good."

"What do you mean?" Maureen spoke.

"Well," he looked a little embarrassed, "I'm getting a bit old for all of this now. Time to do something different."

They all looked at him, expectantly.

"I've bought meself a little bar in Spain. On the beach, y'know. Thought I'd head out there and get some sun. Work for me, for once." He smiled broadly. "This time, I'll be booking the turns!"

"Spain?" The four of them said at once.

"Ooh, how lovely, Mickey." Cooed Barbara.

"That'll be different." Sid said, always unsure of anything foreign.

"I think it's time for something different." Laughed Mickey.

Roger took a step forward and held out his hand towards Mickey.

"All the best, mate. And, well, thank you. You know." Roger coughed, unaccustomed to any sort of public display like this.

Mickey looked surprised, stared at the other man's hand and put down his bag before reaching out to shake it.

"Thanks. Thanks for that." He gripped Roger's hand and smiled.

Mickey picked up his bag and began walking towards a row of cars parked on the roadside. He looked back once at Maureen and smiled.

"All the best to you, too." He opened the car door and threw his bag on the back seat, before laying his suit bag over the top of it.

The four of them watched him climb in his car, start the engine but, before setting off, he wound down the window and waved a final goodbye.

"Send us a postcard!" Called Maureen, waving at him as he roared off down the street.

They watched him turn a corner at the end and they all began to walk towards their digs, Sid and Roger, hands in pockets, while Maureen and Barbara, walked with their arms linked together.

"I've always fancied Spain, you know." Barbara spoke out for all of them to hear.

"Must've made a few bob, if he's buying a bar." Roger replied.

"Ah, cheap as anything over there, you know. All deigo's and dogs." Sid sniffed. "Not for me, Spain. No decent food or drink, all that foreign muck."

"How would you know?" Asked Barbara. "You've never bloody been!"

They all laughed as Sid grumbled.

"Do you think he'll send a postcard?" Asked Barbara. "I'd like to know how he gets on."

"He'd have a job." Said Roger. "He doesn't know where we live!"

They laughed, all except Maureen.

No, she thought, that's the last we'll see of him.

Chapter Thirty-five
End of the Road

Slim stood by the side of the road and watched as his four friends made the last-minute adjustments to their bikes. He was at something of a loss as to what to say.

He was standing with his own bike, bags packed, after they'd spent the morning gathering all of their things together and taking down the tent.

He'd tried to talk them out of it but Billy was adamant. They were leaving.

They'd explained what had happened at the disco when they'd got back to the campsite that night, Slim had dispensed aspirin and a couple of plasters from the first-aid kit his mum had insisted he should take, while he listened to the tale of the fight, the police station and the decision taken in his absence.

He'd refused to go.

"But you can't stay here on your own, Slim." Billy had said.

"But it was nothing to do with me!" Slim had pleaded and begged, but to no avail.

Decisions taken, Slim had wandered off to find a phone box and had called Collette to explain what was happening.

She hadn't been happy that he was leaving so soon but he'd promised her he'd be back the week after. Then she'd cried and it took everything he had not to cry too.

And here they were.

Billy looked up to see Slim standing there, a look of utter misery on his face. He sighed.

"Look, you know it's for the best, Slim. If we stay, we're in trouble. If you're with us, you're an enemy too. It's safer this way."

Slim looked down at his shoes and nodded like a scolded child who knows the parent is right.

"It's only forty miles away Slim," Michael chimed in, "you'll be back here in no time."

Slim just looked away at the road into Bridlington town, like he was never going to see it again.

"And she can always come to York." Billy suggested.

"Yeah, we can show her the sights!" Nutty added, throwing his long leg over the crossbar.

"Sod off." Muttered Slim.

Billy walked over and put his arm around his friend's shoulders.

"Look mate, I'm sorry this happened but it did and we're better at home."

"You might be." He sulked.

Billy walked over to where James was holding his bike and raised his eyebrows in exasperation. James shook his head. They all mounted their bikes, Slim with reluctance and they headed out onto the coast road.

"SLIM! SLIM!" A voice shouted from behind them and they all turned to see Collette running down the road towards them, her hair streaming out behind her, waving her arms at them.

"Jesus!" Cried Nutty.

"Collette!" Slim shouted out. He threw his bike down on the road and he began running towards her, his little legs pumping furiously as his feet slapped the tarmac.

They caught up to each other embraced, broke apart, laughed and embraced again. Slim's shoulders were rising and falling with the effort of running as Collette reached up and stroked his hair, his face and buried her head in his shoulder again.

Billy stood astride his bike, arms leant on the handlebars and smiled.

The others watched the ensuing scene and then turned to him.

"Are we waiting for him then?" Asked Michael.

Billy looked at him and just shook his head.

"No mate. I don't think we are."

Some days later, Roger and Sid pushed their cases into the hold of the coach and stood back to let the driver fasten the door down.

George Rivers was standing by the door, with his clip-board, checking he had everyone, before looking over to them.

"Time to go, you two." He called to them.

They both took a look around at the scenes around them, theirs being one of several coaches being boarded by reluctant factory workers.

The resort was quiet now, the fortnight at an end. Most of the guest houses had 'Vacancies' signs in their windows, ready for the next wave of holiday makers from around the country.

Roger passed Sid a cigarette.

"Ready mate?" Sid asked.

"Aye, I'm ready."

"One for the album this time, eh?"

"Yeah, too true. A fortnight to remember." Roger laughed.

Above them, they heard the rapping of wedding rings on glass, as Maureen and Barbara gestured at them to hurry up.

They turned and smiled up at their wives, who both looked tanned and happy, as they began to make their way to the coach door.

George followed them up the steps and pulled the door closed behind them and, as Roger and Sid made their way to sit down, he called out.

"Right, you lot!"

The chatter of conversation on the coach died as they all turned to look at him.

"We'll be off now, so you better have packed everything 'cos that's it now until we reach York."

A groan of disappointment sounded.

He tapped his clipboard. He hadn't finished.

"However," he added, "when we get to the club, it's not over." Faces turned to him in surprise. "The brewery have put on a buffet and free drinks to welcome us back!"

The coach resounded with cheers and laughter, not to mention a few beer bottles being popped open, everyone keen to make the best of the last few hours of their holiday.

"Have they missed us, George?" Laughed Roger.

"Takings must be well down." Added Sid.

George just smiled in response and took his seat behind the driver.

He tapped him on the shoulder.

"We're ready when you are."

Epilogue
And the hits just keep on coming...

November 1978
York

Maureen padded from the kitchen in her slippers, across the front room towards the door, having heard the letter box rattle and the postman whistling down the street.

The winter sun was only just beginning to break through, a light patter of rain against the glass adding to the gloom as Maureen yawned and pulled her robe around her more tightly against the morning chill.

She saw a few envelopes on the mat and turned them over in her hands. Two were for Roger but there was one for her in a slightly battered envelope that had some foreign stamps on. She couldn't make them out without her glasses. She moved away from the door and walked back to the kitchen to where she had started to make the morning tea. She threw Roger's letters onto the kitchen table and turned the one addressed to her, over and over in her hands.

"Maureen?" Roger's voice called down to her. "Is that tea ready yet?"

"Won't be long!" She called back, still looking at the envelope.

She couldn't make out the postmark but, as the kettle started to rumble on the gas, she tore it open and took out the card that was inside.

It was a postcard from somewhere called Menorca, with pictures of suntanned people in sandy coves.

Turning it over, she recognised the handwriting immediately.

'Dear Maureen, I hope this card finds you well…'

"Oh shit." She breathed.

Printed in Poland
by Amazon Fulfillment
Poland Sp. z o.o., Wrocław